AF119505

The Legend of the Light-Bearers

A Fable about Personal Reinvention and Global Transformation

By Dr. Joe Rubino

The long-awaited prequel to the best-selling personal-development tale, The Magic Lantern: A Fable about Leadership, Personal Excellence, and Empowerment

The Legend of the Light-Bearers:
A Fable about Personal Reinvention and Global Transformation
By Dr. Joe Rubino

Vision Works Publishing,
First Edition Copyright, 2005
By Dr. Joe Rubino
All rights reserved.
Published by Vision Works Publishing
(888) 821-3135 Fax: (630) 982-2134
VisionWorksBooks@Email.com

Manufactured in the United States of America
Reproduction or translation of any part of this book beyond
that permitted by Section 107 or 108 of the 1976 United States
Copyright Act without the permission of the copyright owners
is unlawful. Requests for permission or further information
should be addressed to the Permissions Department,
Vision Works Publishing, P.O. Box 217, Boxford, Massachusetts 01921

ISBN 0-9728840-2-5
Library of Congress Control Number: 2004104732
10 9 8 7 6 5 4 3 2 1

Dedication

This book is dedicated to those who envision a bright and compelling future and have the courage to live passionately in the pursuit of their dreams.

Acknowledgment

Thanks to my mentors in the arena of personal development, Mike Smith and Carol McCall, for inspiring excellence and personal and global transformation.
Thanks also to my editor, Evelyn Howell.
Her creativity and insights grace this book.
Thanks to Steve Kossack for the cover photo.

What People Are Saying:

"Dr. Rubino reduces the complexity, materialism, and divisiveness of modernity into an imaginative fable, giving us direction and wisdom along with an entertaining read."

— Richard D. Lamm
Three-term former Governor of Colorado

"*The Legend of the Light-Bearers* is a magical journey of an enlightened woman who, through her innocence, compassion, and love, brings out the inherent beauty in others and in the world she touches. This fable blends adventure and fantasy with very real messages of peace, harmony, and unity. I know that as you take this journey with Matilda, you will recognize and honor your own journey as a Light-Bearer."

— Lisa Hepner
Author, *Peaceful Earth:
Spiritual Perspectives on Inner Peace and World Peace*

"Dr. Joe Rubino is simply a great story teller. *The Legend of the Light-Bearers* is both timely and much needed. Rubino's ability to weave the intricate tapestries involved in the imaginary world together with an inspirational vision that absolutely compels his audience to aspire to ever higher ambitions, is remarkable."

— Eldon Taylor, Ph.D.
Director, Progressive Awareness Research, Inc.,
Author, *Thinking Without Thinking:
Who's in Control of Your Mind?*

"Dr. Rubino uses his literary genius through this magical and compelling fable as a way of reminding us all of some of the most basic keys to a happy, balanced and satisfying life. If you are still on your journey and in quest of tools to re-invent and re-ignite your inner spirit, this is a great book to gift yourself or anyone you love."

— Constance Dugan
Co-Founder, The Heart of Business

"A simple but profound little book about a girl named Matilda who reconnects us with the deeper truths of our purpose and the amazing way that we are all connected."

— Rachel Conerly
Partner, The Collaborative Institute, Inc.

"*The Legend of the Light-Bearers* is an enchanting parable that speaks to the many lessons our world desperately needs to learn today. It outlines the new paradigm of peaceful cooperation and personal excellence that must replace the need to dominate others, if our world and its people are to grow stronger and thrive."

— Bob Burg
Author, *Winning Without Intimidation*

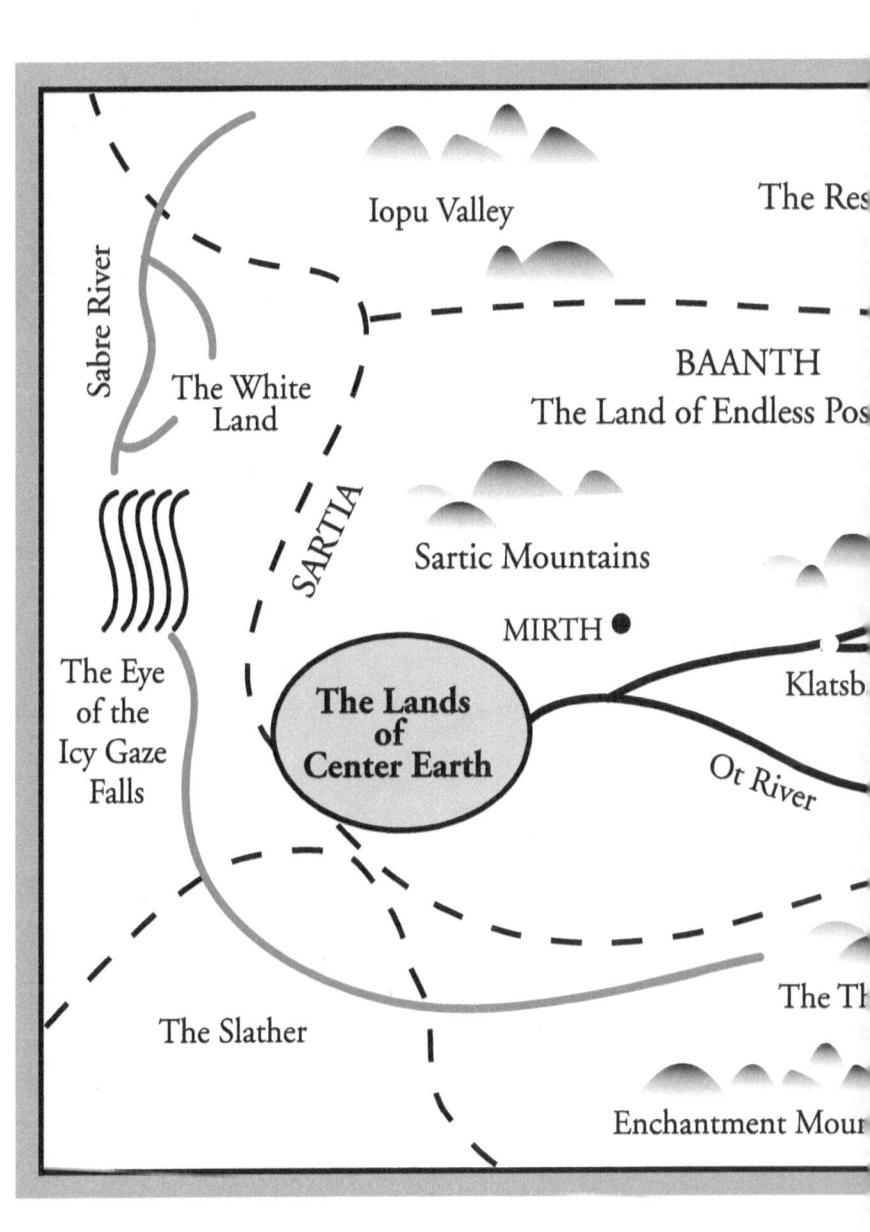

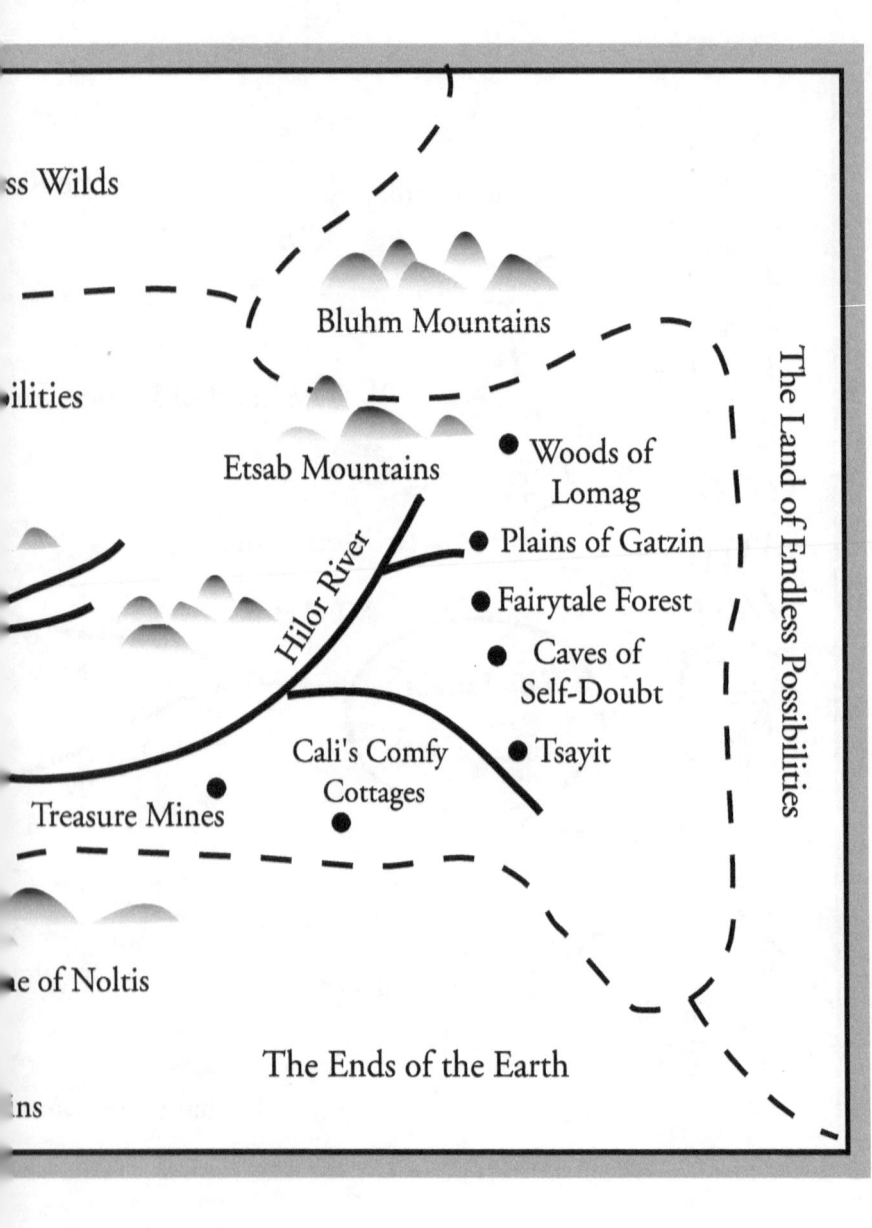

Contents

Chapter 1 .... The Gray Reality .... Page 13

Chapter 2 .... The Visit .... Page 32

Chapter 3 ..... The Passage to Possibilities ...... Page 41

Chapter 4 .... Wiggen's Burden .... Page 56

Chapter 5 .... The Challenge of the Armies ..... Page 69

Chapter 6 .... True North .... Page 79

Chapter 7 ...... The Cave of Addiction .... Page 91

Chapter 8 ...... The Eye of the Icy Gaze ...... Page 103

Chapter 9 ..... The Completion Chamber ..... Page 118

Chapter 10 .... The Slather .... Page 130

Chapter 11 .... The Vision Pool .... Page 145

Chapter 12 ...... The Throne of Noltis .... Page 150

Chapter 13 ...... The Sage of Shelindar .... Page 171

Chapter 14 .. The Light of a New Era Dawns ... Page 185

Chapter 1
The Gray Reality

Matilda awoke at what should have been morning's first light from another long night of restless sleep. She felt like her eyes must have had all their color run out by now from crying so much. Today was her 16th birthday and she was feeling terribly sorry for herself. "What a place to celebrate!" she muttered to herself. As she peered out from the opening of her dark and gloomy cave, she once again struggled to believe she wasn't dreaming as she saw the all-too-familiar pall of bleakness enveloping her tiny, desolate mountainside village. For eight years now, ever since the Earth Change had taken place, a foreboding sense of evil seemed to blanket the survivors' world. They lived in the daily gloom of oppressive heat but without the benefit of any bright sunlight. The air had been fouled and the sun obscured as a result of dark forces that brought about the cataclysm. The previously clean, crisp air that Matilda had known in the early days of her childhood was now replaced by a drab blanket of dark haze that obscured the sun's rays during every hour of the day and night. Every day was the same — just light enough to see but always darkened by perpetual gloom. Without the life-giving energy of the sun's rays, no plant life grew here except mushrooms and a few other forms of fungi.

Life had become both a physical and mental struggle to survive. On too many mornings like this, Matilda and her fellow townspeople found themselves enveloped by fear, struggling to breathe, suffocated by the ominous veil that smothered their already dulled senses.

As she stumbled to her feet, feeling the dry and dusty stone floor of the cave beneath her, Matilda recalled that it was not always like this. Reaching for the gourd on her belt that she used as a water dipper, she felt the tingling of a momentary shiver of joy rush through her spirit as she remembered her life as a young 7-year-old girl. But as she tasted the prior day's warm, stale water from the well bucket, the joyful sensation was quickly gone. During those days before the vast Earth Change, Matilda had lived a happy, carefree life on the edge of the great Western Sea with her loving parents. What a contrast that was to the dry, dark, and lifeless terrain surrounding the labyrinth of caves she and 23 other "lucky" survivors of the disaster now called home. Where there had been the soothing solitude of blue ocean waters with an occasional white-cap riding the horizon, only brown parched and arid land now surrounded her in all directions for as far as her eyes could see. She now realized just how truly blessed her life had been. Although, at the time, she took her good fortune for granted.

Matilda's father, Costas, had been a fisherman back during those lost days that now seemed like another lifetime. She fondly remembered him coming home from his sea journeys. He'd be standing proudly at the wheel of his wooden fishing craft, his kindly face beaming, his bald pate glistening in the sun like a shiny brown egg and his gray chin whiskers jutting stiffly like a wire brush. She recalled with longing how, as a toddler sitting upon his lap, she had reached up her tiny fingers to explore the sun-baked crevices and laugh lines of his leathery face.

Costas was a simple man who loved the sea nearly as much as his family. In better times, to his many friends and strangers alike, he would boast, "What a blessed man I am to have one foot upon the magnificent sea and the other firmly planted on land within the embrace of my loving family."

Though he had set aside each seventh-day to be home from the sea, time to be savored with his beautiful wife, Tonesia, and their daughter, Matilda, too many work days in the sun had often blistered his forehead and the salty seawater would constantly burn his chapped hands. Looking out over the dried plain that had once been the sea floor, how he wished for the stinging slap of wind-driven waves. Now, with the sky a perpetual and foreboding gray, how he longed for the sun's warmth upon his weathered skin. He had had no choice but to make the caves their new home, settle and constantly grub for anything edible to stave off starvation. For eight years now, he had labored to live a new life, but it felt like the desperate life of a gasping fish stranded on the beach. Often Costas would grumble, "I feel like I'm covered with barnacles from tip to toe and can't stay afloat." He swore he would never get used to the unforgiving hardness of the stone floor that daily wreaked havoc upon his tired, old arthritic joints. At times, watching him, Matilda thought that she could measure his sadness by the pound. His body seemed to double over beneath the heavy shadow of the new world's doom. Contorted and broken in body and spirit, he would limp from barren bush to barren tree in his daily search for the hidden fungi and burrowing insects that they all relied upon for food — the only other things that survived without sunlight. "Ah, what I'd give for a bowl of fish chowder!" he mumbled, thinking to himself about how much he now missed the plentiful seafood he had once grown weary of eating.

Fishing and family had been the cornerstones of Costas' life, leaving no room for interest in faraway political matters or in the quarrels among his country's leaders and those of foreign lands. Certainly, the idea that any country's top politicians had conducted secret underground tests of terrible, deadly weapons had never entered the fisherman's simple and practical mind. Now, old beyond his 62 years, Costas knew himself to be a beaten man, an empty shell that questioned the sanity of keeping up the daily struggle to stay alive.

"I feel like the great storm has washed away my spirit, leaving only the driftwood of my body behind on the shore," Matilda often heard him say. Only one reason remained for his dogged perseverance: Matilda. As he struggled in fear and sadness to care for her, Costas wondered how those in charge could have cared so little to not have foreseen the outcome of their selfish power plays.

Costas and Matilda shared their labyrinth of mountain caves with 23 other equally hard-pressed surviving villagers. Eight years before, in panic they had all scrambled up to what had seemed to be their mountain sanctuary.

"Some sanctuary!" Costas often grumbled at the village meetings. "Life here in this horrible place is so much more difficult than it used to be. So much knowledge from the Great Halls of Learning is now lost to us. Even the simplest tasks, like drawing water from the underground stream, is so much more challenging here. In the old days, with the technology we had, an engine could have done the work of 20 mules. Perhaps the many who died in the Earth Change are now better off than we are."

And yet, deep in his heart, he knew better than that. He actually was grateful for being chosen as one of the blessed few who survived and remembered to give thanks each night for this miracle in his prayers with Matilda. Nevertheless, his gratitude did not prevent him from venting his anger in his daily morning ritual of exiting their cave and shaking his fist angrily at the darkened sky and shouting "Dark forces!"

Whatever good fortune was his, Costas knew that he owed much of it to Tonesia, his beloved wife, who was tragically lost during the catastrophic Earth Change. It seemed like only yesterday that she had asked him to take Matilda up the mountain in search of he huan pi, the "happiness herb." She had instructed him that this rare herb was found in the bark of the pinyanni trees that grew only in the northernmost reaches of the Red Rock Mountains.

Tonesia had long studied the healing arts under the tutelage of the revered mountain medicine man, Esia. As was the custom to honor her mentor and the wisdom he had shared, she had changed her name to "Tonesia," meaning "I sing the song of Esia." It conveyed to others that she too was on the path to become a wise and spiritual healer.

As a restorer of health, Tonesia had often used huan pi and other herbs to help relieve the suffering bodies and burdened minds of any who came to her, and over the years, Tonesia had helped many to find healing and fulfillment.

She was a radiant beauty, inside and out, whose joy would spill forth as music. Costas recalled how her singing filled any room she entered with melodious harmony. If he closed his eyes, he could still see her long black hair lifted by the breeze as she stood, knee-deep in the balmy green waves splashing along the shore, humming a homecoming tune that welcomed his return from the sea. Tonesia *was* his world. And now she was gone. Tears welled in his eyes. He felt like a dam weakening before the force of a raging torrent.

They had first met at the home of a friend. Yes, her physical beauty had drawn him to her, but even more alluring were her warm, generous heart and charismatic ways. Costas sensed from the start that Tonesia was a healer, even before the years of study that caused her to fully realize her extraordinary gift. As news of her ability to heal spread, suffering people would journey from far away. Tonesia refused all credit for her healing touch and wise counsel, swearing she was but the vessel to teach others to realize their own inner healing powers. Now, tired of the struggle and distraught about the future, Costas felt a wave of shame deep from within his soul. He knew Tonesia would have led these villagers to a better life, had she survived in his stead. But unfortunately he was not Tonesia, and for this he despaired.

Matilda greeted Costas on this new day as cheerily as she could. "Good morning, Father," she said and tried to give a broad smile to conceal her own inner sadness. She felt her father's pain along with the unceasing love he had always shared with her. And today once would have been a most special day.

"And a good morning and very happy birthday to you, Tildie!" he offered in return. "How does it feel to turn 16?"

"Good, I guess," Matilda answered.

"Well, let's start your 16th birthday off right!" Costas encouraged. He pulled a small silk pouch from his pocket and handed it to his daughter with great care. "Happy birthday, my best girl."

Matilda opened the pouch to reveal a curiously shaped amulet hung on a fine chain of almost thread-like gold. "Why, it's beautiful!" she exclaimed as she held it up by its chain.

"It was your mother's," Costas explained gruffly. He placed the chain around her neck so that the amber nugget hung over her heart. "We had planned to surprise you with it on your 16th birthday. Many years ago, when you were just a little girl, your mother asked me to keep it with me at all times until this special day arrived."

"Why, thank you so much, Father! I will never be without it from this day forward." Matilda leaned up to kiss his cheek, noting with a pang that her father seemed to shrink a little every day.

Blinking back tears, Costas coughed and searched for a way to change the subject. "Where's that great golden sweetheart of yours?" he asked, turning to look for the shaggy hound that was Matilda's constant companion.

"Shire's out romping in the brush," Matilda answered. "Not even dark forces or perpetual gloom can dampen her spirits!" Shire was strong-willed and high-spirited, and vitality seemed to surge from her floppy ears and silky golden coat. Matilda had rescued the stranded pup after the Earth Change. Matilda decided to name her "Shire" after a green and abundant country she had read about in her studies of foreign lands. Shire gave Matilda joy. Her frisky play helped ease the drudgery of survival in this harsh, new world. The tedious daily search for food consumed most of Matilda's day, when she wasn't hauling water buckets or collecting sticks for the fire. Shire buoyed Matilda's spirits time and again.

But today, as a young lady of 16, Matilda knew she must finally face the most serious of matters. "Tell me the full story, Father, about how our world was devastated," she pleaded.

Costas hobbled back to the boulder where Matilda sat. He put his arm around her and gave her a tight hug. "Very well," he said slowly, but he closed his eyes as if in pain before speaking again. "It's about time for you to know the whole story." He again stopped speaking with a great sigh. Matilda waited, wondering if this might be one tale too hard to put into words. Costas finally heaved his wide shoulders with another heavy sigh. "No, Tildie. I am but a simple fisherman, and these matters were always beyond my comprehension. Let us go and ask the Augur."

Accepting that this answer was the best he could give her, Matilda grasped her father's arm and supported him as they left their cave. Down the dusty trail they came to a lower landing where a small opening was carved out of the rocky mountainside. "Oh, Knowing One, may we approach?" Costas called into the darkness.

"Of course. You are always welcome!" called back the old woman known as the Augur. Slowly, the glow of her torch came into view, as a tiny but sturdy old woman came to the entrance.

"Oh, All-Mother, thank you!" Costas greeted the old woman with the courtesy due her many years. The oldest of all the villagers, the Augur was esteemed as a wise, honorary mother. No one recalled her name or how many years she had lived. "My daughter Tildie, ahem, Matilda today welcomes her 16th year and yearns for knowledge about the Earth Change. I am a simple man, so we come to you for greater understanding," Costas beseeched, his head bowed low in respect.

The Augur was more than ancient. All knew she possessed great learning, wisdom, and insight. She understood history better than anyone alive, both before and after the Earth Change. Fewer people knew that she also possessed the gift of prophesy, because she rarely shared her visions of the future, thinking that doing so might rob them of valuable lessons to be learned. What none of the villagers had ever known was that the Augur was the last of a race rumored to live for more than 300 years; now all of them had passed on. During her younger years and the time of her peak influence, the Augur had counseled many with integrity and wisdom. Once she had taught in the esteemed Halls of Learning as a respected master, a voice of reason and trusted advisor to the highest leaders. She had retired to the village and continued giving her wise counsel for generations. After the Earth Change, it was the Augur who told the survivors how to find water and dig a well, how to find food, to build a fire, to make torches. Without her, all would have surely perished.

The Augur embraced Costas and smiled warmly at Matilda. Pointing to a low, wide ledge by her cave, she said, "Please sit and be welcome. I shall do my best to relay these matters as I know them. For the past 50 years, our world has witnessed the rule of many selfish and corrupt tyrants. Too many. They claimed to rule with the best interests of their people in mind, but they were greedy. They hungered for money, glory, and power. Power most of all. These rulers used power to dominate others. They trusted no one because they knew that their own dark hearts could not be trusted. Always suspicious that others were plotting to control or overthrow them, they started delving into secret knowledge, dark knowledge of destruction and fear. These secrets opened our world to dark forces that could be wielded to kill throngs of people in the blink of an eye."

"But I was taught in school that such forces were only used as threats that surely would *scare* people into their senses," Matilda burst out.

"Maybe that was the way some meant it to work," the Augur answered. "But they forgot that dark forces have their own will and a thirst for control. Many factions fought to expand their power and to dominate their neighbors."

"But how could people like that be trusted with such weapons?" Matilda wondered.

"That's precisely the problem: They could not be trusted. Their excessive knowledge of things best left unknown overwhelmed any good intentions."

"How could anyone tell which side was the right side if they all used evil powers to hurt each other?" Matilda interrupted.

Costas shook his head from side to side.

"Your father is indeed correct," the Augur affirmed. "That was just another means of justifying hurtful behavior that sought to tyrannize others."

"But didn't anyone stand up for peace and sensibility?" Matilda prompted.

"A few like me did, but our voices were squelched by the cries of those who instilled fear and hatred in the people," she continued. "Before anyone truly realized the magnitude of the destructive forces that were multiplying, it was too late."

"So how did the Earth Change actually come about?" Matilda asked.

"We don't know exactly who was responsible for tilting the scale," the Augur answered. "But I sensed a surge of dimensional energy that could only mean that some force from outside our plane of existence was allowed into our world. The resultant disruptions expanded the plates that held the Earth intact. Where the fault lines widened, parts of the Earth's surface caved in. Many vanished with the fallen lands."

"But how did our village get swept away? It didn't fall in," Matilda said in a shaky voice.

"When the Earth collapsed inward, the great oceans' waters shifted with them and deluged many of the previously dry lands. What was once covered by the sea then rose up or became exposed and formed new land and mountain ranges through the distortion of the Earth's crust."

"Standing high on the mountainside that day, we could see the ocean rise up in a monstrous wave and flood the shore," Costas said with a shudder. "We saw and could do nothing. And so Tonesia was swept away in an instant."

"And those of us in the mountains survived, but why were *we* saved? There has to be a reason that we're still here and my mother is gone," Matilda persisted.

The Augur looked at Matilda with loving pity. "Ah, but sometimes we never learn the reason for the pain life brings. Sometimes the answer is before our eyes, but our minds are too young and small to understand. We have no way of knowing if others survived elsewhere as well. If so, did they live for the same reason that we did? Why any of us were saved, that answer I don't have to give you."

"Could it be because we were destined to carry on and rebuild our world from this disaster?" Matilda asked. "I see this just might be our mission and our destiny."

"You sound just like your mother! I'd love to believe that, Matilda," Costas countered. "But I see no evidence for that bold statement. We are trapped in this world without light and hope, and here we die. The dark forces have won!"

Costas shook his head in disgust, tersely thanked the Augur for sharing her insights, and limped down the mountainside trail to start the day's chore of picking fungi. Before he was lost to sight, Matilda and the Augur saw him shake his fist angrily at the sky and curse "Dark forces!" as he was wont to do.

Matilda considered her father's pessimistic words. Her intuition told her there had to be hope and light in their future.

"Have faith. Know that it is all good," reassured the Augur. "Even those happenings that bring us suffering and heartache have their purpose. We just may not know that purpose yet. However, I can say that I see grand things in your future. You will have great protection wherever you go. Remember this: There is still magic and promise to be had in this realm and beyond it, if you have the courage to pursue it. Go now and be glad."

Pressing the old woman's hands gratefully in hers, Matilda thanked the Augur and then retreated back up the path to her cave. She felt a deep need to rest and reflect upon what the Augur had revealed. What did she mean by beyond this realm, she wondered?

Upon reaching her cave, Matilda threw herself down on her bedroll. She closed her eyes and tumultuous thoughts of days past rushed to fill her mind like a sea flooding adjacent caves at high tide. How she longed to return to the blessed times she had shared with Tonesia and Costas and their neighbors in their village by the sea. She could hear her mother's voice say to her, "Remember, my darling, open your heart and always trust your intuition, for it is never wrong." Clinging to that small reassurance and the Augur's hopeful promise, Matilda shut out the apparent hopelessness of her world's situation. She curled up like a cat in the shade trying to avoid the heat of an oppressive summer day, and in a few moments, her breathing sang with the rhythm of healing sleep.

Chapter 2
The Visit

It seemed that Matilda had been sleeping only a short while when a familiar song stirred the air and awakened her. A thrill ran down her spine as she recognized her mother's favorite tune being sung in her mother's voice. "I must be once again dreaming of my mother like I have done so many times before," Matilda muttered but still opened her eyes to look for her mother as if, just this once, the dream would be true. As she blinked the sleep from her eyes, Matilda was startled to see a shadowy figure standing there before her. A shadow, but Matilda still recognized Tonesia's familiar, tender loving smile as she crooned her melody.

Though first a shadow and then almost translucent, her mother otherwise appeared unchanged. She wore a flowing gossamer gown and her long, black hair fluttered in the breeze, although the air in the cave was still. Tonesia embraced Matilda, long and lovingly.

Although she could no longer feel a physical touch, Matilda felt her mother's love as strongly as ever. All of the pain and sadness ebbed away.

Matilda took a half-step back to gaze into her mother's eyes. "But how can this be?" she whispered in disbelief.

Tonesia said, "The talisman you wear around your neck has special powers indeed. By donning it on this special day, you have altered certain energies and shifted dimensions, allowing me to appear before you. By wearing my charm, you have reaffirmed our unbreakable bond to each other and summoned me to your side. Though I have always been with you, you now can feel my presence more closely. Do you not know that we can never be truly separated, my dear one? Death is merely an illusion that allows us to experience more and learn from the emotional journey we ourselves have chosen. I have returned to assure you that you will always possess a special knowing within. You will always have access to the answers you seek. You only need look inside to find them. Know too that my spirit will be with you always. You need mourn my death no more. We shall be together always, in this realm and beyond."

"I have listened to what the Augur had to say about the Earth Change, but I am still perplexed. Please, help me to understand why this had to happen," Matilda pleaded.

Tonesia continued, "You, your villagers, and many others you don't yet know have survived the great Earth Change for a reason. The world had grown ugly, and evil had overcome goodness. People had become self-absorbed, obsessed with power and the need for domination. Men forgot that their lifetimes on Earth were finite and not all-important in the grand scheme of things. Love and generosity were forgotten concepts in many corners of the globe. Greed and control flourished. Men forgot who they really were and succumbed to their destructive emotions. Anger consumed their hearts like an old jack pine tree covered in so much moss that you can no longer see the tree."

"How could the situation have gotten so out of control, Mother?" Matilda interrupted.

Tonesia smiled and went on, "Anger is a mighty force, more addicting than the strongest herb. Angry men willingly traded rationality, love, and care for others for the power of manipulating and controlling others."

"Even if it meant suffering, death, and destruction for all?" Matilda asked.

"Yes. They were totally blind to the costs of their actions," Tonesia agreed. "If they could not dominate others and not avoid being dominated, life was not worth living. Their anger also sought to make the most of the emotion of fear. The more innocent lives they claimed, the more fear they generated, but they told themselves that their anger was righteous, that they were *right* to pursue and destroy any enemy. And the definition of an enemy was anyone who embraced an opposing philosophy."

"So it really came down to each side becoming obsessed with the need to be right, needing to dominate others and justify their own righteous anger," Matilda blurted. "How dare they do that!"

"Yes, 'how dare they' is exactly right, Matilda. It's what each side said about the other. Each was unwilling to put themselves in the other person's world and generate any empathy for the other's position. This insistence on being right allowed them to shun any possible peaceful resolutions to their differences and resort to hatred and violence instead," Tonesia added. "That world chose darkness and hate over light and love. It is for this reason that the Earth Change and planetary cleansing were necessary. The perpetual gloom you have seen in the sky since the great upheaval is the residue of that hatred from the dark forces, still enveloping your world. It will continue as a reminder until the day that those in the new world renounce anger, hatred, and fear and take a stand for light, love, and harmony."

"But it all seems so terribly hopeless! How can we rebuild our world upon these principles of love and restore the sun's healing light to our planet?" Matilda wondered aloud.

"By initiating change so that it might happen," Tonesia answered. "By sharing this possibility with others who will also spread the change, until the world knows of love's potential impact. You, my darling girl, must lead this quest to rid the world of gloom. You will find the source of your strength inside you. The situation is anything but hopeless if you have faith and keep the hope alive. You will have the power of good on your side and will find the world to possess magical gifts awaiting your discovery."

"How is it that you know all this, Mother? Where did you gain such wisdom and magic?" Matilda asked.

"My transformation began while I was in physical form on Earth. My education with my mentor set me on my healing path. My powers as a medicine woman allowed me to contribute to the lives of many then. My powers were greatly increased when my body passed into shadow. I have learned a great deal from other, wiser teachers and guides here."

With a wave of her hand, Tonesia continued, "This day is a special one for you, my dear. Not only does it mark your 16th birthday, but it represents your initiation into our healers' circle. Great things lie ahead for you! Now, look again at your birthday gift! You will find that it is much more than just an attractive trinket."

Matilda closely examined the amulet that hung around her neck. "Why it's a tinder box!" she exclaimed.

"Yes, a magic tinder box," her mother said.

Matilda struck the tinder box and a small flame was ignited. The flame was small but within seconds, its light filled the entire cave with a warm and loving glow, echoing the hopeful love Matilda now felt healing her broken heart.

"You have an inner fire that has not yet been lit," Tonesia counseled. "Resignation is so unnecessary and serves no one. You have already seen that. The world relies upon your quest to spread this light and vanquish the ever-present gloom. My intuition tells me that this is your life purpose. You can not fail."

"My life purpose?" Matilda repeated, pondering the words and their implications. "I'm not even sure I have a life purpose."

"Why, of course you do. We all do. But we must each discover it and declare it for all to hear and be inspired," Tonesia continued. "Would you like to discover it now?"

"Oh, yes. That would be the greatest birthday present I could ever imagine!" Matilda pleaded.

"Very well, then. What have you always loved to do? What have you always been known for as a child, before losing hope?"

"Well, I always have loved brainstorming possibilities and inspiring people to see things they may not have seen clearly before," Matilda said.

"And what do you think the world needs most these days?"

"Why, that's easy. The world needs to rid itself of this pervasive gloom and fear."

Tonesia nodded. "And what is the antidote to gloom and fear?"

"Light and love, of course."

"And what could you spend the next 300 years doing so that you'd jump up from bed each day, so excited about getting started?" Tonesia queried.

"Spreading light and love!" Matilda confirmed convincingly.

"So, what is your life purpose?" Tonesia asked.

"Why, to rid the world of gloom and spread light and love. That rings true for me. But where do I start?" Matilda pleaded.

Tonesia smiled in the way only a mother can and said, "Start at the beginning. Know that you will have great assistance and that your answers lie within. You possess an inner wisdom that awaits your discovery. I love you and will be with you always. Call on me and somewhere deep inside you, you will always find an answer. There is still much light, love, and magic to be revealed in the world. You will be a *source* for these gifts to be revealed."

"What do you mean when you say that I will be a source?" Matilda asked.

"Through your leadership, others will find their answers. They will reconnect with love. Light will fill their souls, the gloom will vanish, and the world will transform, as if by magic. And all that will spring from things that you do."

With these words, Tonesia disappeared.

Chapter 3
The Passage to Possibilities

Matilda stood for a moment, frozen in shock. She had been overcome with joy at the appearance of her mother, but now her mother was gone again, leaving Matilda with that horrible, empty feeling of loss and abandonment.

"How could you leave so soon? How could you leave me?" Matilda moaned. The pain overwhelmed her. But she could still hear her mother's reassuring words, "Know that you will have great protection and assistance and that your answers lie within. I love you and will be with you always." She would force back the pain with the strength of those promises.

As she made this resolution, her attention was called to the far reaches of the cave. Shire had felt thoroughly ignored for the entire morning, so she had started on her own adventure. Curious as always and a top-notch digger, the golden dog had been exploring beyond the cave's rear wall. Now she was barking with increasing excitement to share her discovery. Matilda grabbed her torch and ran toward Shire's yelps. To her astonishment, Shire had dug under a large rock formation until the soil had collapsed into a much deeper cavern. In those distant depths, Matilda heard the rushing waters of a subterranean stream. As she cautiously edged nearer for a better look, the earth below their feet gave way. Matilda and her dog found themselves falling down the expanding sink hole. After falling for what seemed like an eternity, Matilda and Shire landed with ferocious force into a deep pool. As they struggled back up to the surface, the stream's powerful current swept Matilda and Shire onward like a pair of leaves.

Further and further down they tumbled, deeper and deeper beneath the mountain. The water kept filling their noses and mouths, until Matilda feared they'd be drowned. Finally, she and Shire came to rest, bruised and winded, upon a sandy shore. Although far below the Earth's surface, there seemed to be a vaulted sky, but it held the same gloom.

Matilda sat up and brushed the sand from her tattered clothing and from Shire's coat.

"That was a close call, girl!" she gasped. "You and your digging! Now, how are we going to get out of this mess? At least we're not hurt, I suppose." She sighed and started to look around and get their bearings. But a sudden, fierce buzzing by her ear made her jerk back. She recognized the sound of an arrow's flight. Seconds later, another arrow whizzed by Shire's tail. Matilda dropped down on all fours, grabbed Shire by the tail, and lunged for cover behind a large boulder. From that relative safety, she spied a thin man clad in a yellow tunic and leggings. He knelt behind a tree across the river from her on the farther bank.

"Where are we? Why are you shooting at us?" she yelled in disbelief. "We've done nothing to you!"

"It's not you I'm shooting at, missy," the man scolded in reply.

Matilda spun to look behind her. No more than 10 feet away was an angry, bearded man dressed in blue overalls. He was poking his head out from the bear hole where he was hiding in the side of the cliff bordering the river bank. As Matilda caught sight of him, he stuck his upper body further from the hole and let fly an arrow at the man in yellow.

"I'll get you, you scoundrel!" he yelled as he fired.

"Wait a minute!" Matilda continued. "I repeat, where are we?"

The man with the yellow shirt shouted back "You're now here with all us miserable wretches in the gloomhole we call Center Earth." With these words, he shot another arrow in the direction of his enemy, again nearly missing Shire.

Desperate, Matilda hugged Shire closer behind the boulder. "We must do something – but what? Mother, please help me!"

Matilda clutched the amulet around her neck and remembered her mother's departing words, "Call on me and somewhere deep inside you, you will always find an answer. The world relies upon your quest to spread this light. This is your life purpose. You can not fail." In that instant, it was as if the entire world froze. Matilda's insight hit her with the force of a branch separating a rider from her horse.

"Why of course! I must be the source of light for these combatants. Have I not dealt successfully with arguments before? Certainly, I know how to deal with a situation like this! How foolish of me not to have realized this before!" Matilda almost shook with her excitement.

"Just be *the source*," Matilda reminded herself with a smile. She knew just what to do. At the top of her lungs, she shouted to both men, "Wise sirs, might I suggest a way for you to reach to another outcome besides death and destruction?"

"There is no other outcome," yelled back the man in yellow.

"It's I kill him or he kills me," added the other. "A simple natural law!"

"But what if there was a *different* way?" Matilda pleaded. "Would you both at least be willing to consider the possibility for a few moments? I'm certain I can show you a way!"

"I doubt it!" scowled the man in the cliffside. "Our people have been fighting *his* people for thousands of years, and I don't think we're about to stop now."

"He's evil…and stubborn, as you can see! But I'd be willing to listen… if he is," the other conceded.

"Very well then," Matilda said. "I propose a short truce to simply explore other possibilities. Is that agreeable?"

"Yes, very well, I agree," the man in the yellow shirt said.

"I suppose I do also," offered the bearded man.

"Oh splendid," Matilda said with a great relief. "Drop your weapons and let's meet at this boulder to have our discussion."

Both men slowly put down their bows and walked over to the boulder to join Matilda and Shire.

"Now, by way of introduction, let's each take a turn telling each other a little bit about ourselves. My parents taught me that the first step in dealing with strangers is to develop rapport and explore what we have in common. For example, where are you from? Do you have families? What do you do for a living? And what are you known for and passionate about?" Matilda proceeded to create safety in a way that would have persuaded even the most reluctant participant to open up and share.

"Please allow me to go first. My name is Matilda, daughter of Costas and Tonesia, recently of the Red Rock Mountains. I am 16 years old, and since the Earth Change, I've lived with my father and other survivors in some gloomy caves in our gloomy world, above wherever it is I am now. Before then, I lived by the Western Sea with my parents. My mother's physical body perished with the Earth Change, but she lives on with me in spirit. I recently discovered that my life purpose is to vanquish the gloom that seems to always be present everywhere and spread light and love. But I have no idea how I am going to fulfill my mission yet, so I am open to any suggestions you both may have."

"Get another mission!" said the man with the beard.

"I agree; you're bound to fail!" added the one with the yellow shirt.

Matilda ignored their cynical comments and plowed valiantly on. "It is a pleasure to meet you both, in spite of the challenging circumstances in which we met. But, somehow, I've landed in the middle of this predicament and I have no idea how to get back home. Maybe, if you could stop fighting for a while, you might be able to help me figure things out. I suppose that's enough about me for now," Matilda concluded with a sigh. "If we are to make any progress in resolving your differences, we need to hear from *you* both! You, sir, with the beard, please go next."

"Well, young miss, I'll do my best — since I said so and because I'm a man of my word. My name is Barnaby and I am the son of Gretas and Baylot of the

Ishites in the world above. I landed here in this place we all decided to call Center Earth after the Earth Change — which our enemy, the Plabians caused!" Barnaby glared at his adversary.

"That's a blatant lie!" countered the other man.

Barnaby ignored his outburst and continued, "I live here in the Iopu Valley with my wife, Brefta, and son, Wiggen. Somehow the dark energy released at the time of the Earth Change shriveled the life in my poor son's body. He was only 8 years old at the time. Wiggen's growth was immediately stunted, and he somehow became a dwarf. In fact, he became one of the first of the dwarf children to grow up in this sorry new land. For this, I blame the Plabians!"

"Now wait just a minute," objected the other man. "My people had nothing to do with causing the great Earth Change. We all know that the cataclysm was brought about by the Ishites."

Matilda interrupted, "I can appreciate your perspective, sir, and you will get your chance to speak freely. But for now, allow Barnaby to finish his piece."

"Thank you, Matilda," Barnaby continued. "I am a farmer by trade, and someday, after we annihilate all the remaining Plabians, I hope to return to the land. I am passionate about my family and will do whatever I must to protect them," he concluded.

"Thank you, Barnaby," Matilda said to the bearded man. "What I hear is that you are a loving family man and that the terrible Earth Change dealt great hardship to you and your family. I also heard your love and concern for your son. I understand that you are a farmer, not a warrior, but you fight because of the hurt you feel you were made to endure. Am I right?"

"Yes, miss, you rightly are," Barnaby replied proudly, honored by her understanding.

"Thank you, kind sir. Now, let us hear from this other man."

The man in yellow nervously cleared his throat and said, "I am Cromeas, son of Colun and Reini of the Plabian people. We, too, landed in this world with the disruption of lands in the world above. And, I too, have a dwarfen child, my daughter Kuchina, so I feel your pain, Barnaby! But my people and I must bear the resentment and anger inflicted by those Ishites. We know no other life than to avenge the deaths of our comrades at the hands of our enemies."

"This we share in common," Barnaby shot back.

Cromeas continued, "I now live with my people in the high cliffs of Anatera in the land they call the Restless Wilds. I was once a herald in the world above, and I took pride in my ability to communicate powerfully. When our war is over, I wish to rejoin my family and village and teach them to be great communicators." Cromeas nodded politely to Matilda and took a step backward, indicating he had finished.

"Thank you, Cromeas," Matilda responded. "I heard that you, too, love your family. You have been grievously hurt by the Earth Change and are really a peace-loving man, caught up in an ancient struggle beyond your personal control. I also see you and Barnaby share the tragedy of how your children were affected by the changes."

"You are correct, Matilda," responded Cromeas. "After the lands fell from the world above, most of our children were affected in ways we don't fully understand. They simply stopped growing and developed the same physical features that true dwarves have. Many babies born here since then were also born as dwarves."

"And that's not the worst of it! The foul energy also caused a rise in hostilities between our people. I think people became numb to the horrors of killing other people, " Barnaby added.

"I understand," Matilda shook her head. "Here is a possibility I see. May I offer it?"

Both men nodded in agreement.

Matilda continued, "I see that you both have suffered greatly, and it is only natural to be angry about your suffering. I see that many would agree that you are both good men, doing the best you know how in dealing with a terrible situation. I also see that you both are *not* fond of killing and warfare, but you both long for your peaceful occupations. I actually see you both share much more than what separates you!"

"Yes, I suppose I would agree," Barnaby nodded.

"Me, too," Cromeas grudgingly added.

"Very well," Matilda said. She stopped to think for a minute, not quite sure what to say. As she considered her next words, Matilda instinctively reached up and touched the magic tinder box hanging at her neck. In an instant, a bright light pierced the immediate gloom surrounding both men. Dazzled and stunned, they stared into each other's eyes, almost in a trance. And somehow in this daze, Barnaby found he was no longer looking into Cromeas' eyes. He somehow could see what Cromeas had always seen. He felt Cromeas' love for his family and his people and realized he truly did hate war, although he knew no other way. He saw a remembered scene where Cromeas was 5 years old, sitting upon his grandfather's lap as the elder Plabian warned him, "Listen well, my child. You either kill the Ishites or they will kill you. You have no other option." In a rush, Barnaby understood what Cromeas thought and felt, what it was like to walk in his shoes. He saw that Cromeas was doing the very best he knew how to do based upon the way he was raised to mistrust the Ishites. "I bet Cromeas' grandfather had been told the same," Barnaby mumbled to himself.

During this same time, Cromeas was seeing the world through Barnaby's eyes. "No wonder they hated us!" he thought. "Look at the harm we've inflicted on them as a people for so many years!"

And so each saw the world through the other's eyes and saw the world anew as if for the first time.

Matilda continued, "I am moved by what can happen when we look at each other's world through our hearts and not our egos. With your newfound empathy, what if we could bring light where there was darkness and love where there was hatred? What if we could shift the pattern of violence and actually see your similarities, not your differences? And what if we could build even more upon these bonds? You could actually be the source of a new way of living, a way that rejects war and hatred and embraces peace."

"But our peoples have vowed retribution for so very long. I'm afraid it is all they know!" Barnaby said, shaking his head in regret.

"Yes, but must we blindly continue in the tradition of hatred and suffering just because those who went before us did so?" Cromeas wondered.

"Not if you both decide that it ends here and now. That is *if* you have the courage to forge a new way," Matilda challenged.

"But where would we start? How could two ordinary folks reverse a trend of generations and the hatred of so many people?" Barnaby asked, almost afraid to hope.

"And how could two, or even three people, impact the lives of an entire people?" Cromeas added.

Matilda smiled. "My mother would say, 'Start at the beginning and be the source of the changes you wish to see in the world.' After all, you know the riddle — 'How do you eat an elephant?'"

"One bite at a time!" Barnaby and Cromeas exclaimed in unison.

"Very well then. Let us commit to pursue this new vision for ourselves and our world," Matilda added with joy.

A warm and brilliant glow emanated from all three, slicing through the gloom that had weighed heavy in the air only minutes before. Somehow compelled by this new inner glow, Matilda reached for one of the spent arrows at their feet and snapped off the tip. She tore a strip of cloth from her sleeve and wrapped the arrow shaft with it, then lit it with her tinder box. The torch light drew strength from Cromeas', Barnaby's, and Matilda's inner lights and somehow glowed stronger than any torch had ever done before. The glow lifted their hearts as the gloom in the air surrounding them was banished in an instant. Taking the torch, Matilda lit a long-abandoned, rusty old lantern she found half-buried in the sand. She hung it high on the hillside, and the sooty smoke from the lantern spelled out the following message against the brightened sky:

To influence another with integrity, one must develop rapport, look for areas of mutuality, and seek to contribute to his or her life—without attachment to personal gain.

Chapter 4
Wiggen's Burden

For a brief moment, the three new friends sitting together on the shore shared a spirit of glee. Shire, too, felt their joy, and her golden tail wagged wildly in excitement. Then suddenly, Barnaby became somber again. "But what about my poor son, Wiggen?" he asked. "How can we help him? He's my greatest worry. He's always been so troubled, and now, well, the doctors say he's dying."

Matilda struggled to think of something to say that might comfort Barnaby. Cromeas clumsily clapped Barnaby's shoulder and forced some cheer into his voice, which seemed to get stuck in his throat. "Perhaps Matilda can tell us more about her quest and maybe she can help young Wiggen!" Cromeas suggested.

"Yes, please tell us more," Barnaby agreed.

Matilda paused for a minute in thought. "Well, actually I'm quite puzzled right now. I'm in this strange land. I've left my father in the world above and have no idea how to return there. He must surely be worried sick about me. But my mother always said, 'The best way to take your mind off of your own troubles is to focus on helping others with theirs!' And that actually leads me to the topic of my life purpose. It was only yesterday that I actually discovered that I even had a life purpose. So, it's all still sort of fuzzy in my mind. I know it involves ridding the world of gloom and spreading light and love, but how I'm not sure. I also now know that I must be a beacon of light for myself as I support others to find their own inner light. Again, I'm not sure just how I can make this happen — let alone help Wiggen. I just don't know, Barnaby."

"Say more about how you can support people to find their inner light," Barnaby encouraged.

"Well, I've always loved inspiring people to be their best," Matilda replied. "When they are being their best, they're happy and fulfilled and sharing their happiness with others."

"That's very valuable," Cromeas commented. "Besides the obvious gloom hanging heavy in the air, how do you know when they're living in darkness?"

"If they see war as a necessity, live in poverty, or feel hatred and suffering, that's about as dark as you get." Matilda said. "I'd love to shift their thinking to one of abundance, contribution, love, and harmony."

She went on, "They are also in darkness when they are not being their best, but are resigned to living at less than their potential. I'd love to be able to show them that they need not settle for less."

"It looks to me like you're off to a great start by helping us find our inner light. Perhaps you can become even clearer about your mission by visiting the apparition stream," Barnaby suggested.

"What's that?" Matilda asked with a ripple of eagerness.

"The apparition stream is a magical place where people gain great insights into their lives, past, present, and future," Cromeas told her. "There just may be an apparition awaiting your discovery there!"

"That sounds like a plan," Matilda shouted, jumping to her feet. "Please take me there."

And so the three headed off down the river. People often visited the stream, but with nervous trepidation, unsure of what apparitions might greet them. Within a short time, the trio reached the point where the slowly flowing apparition stream joined the rushing river.

"This is the place," Cromeas was saying when the stream before them glazed over. All three expected to see something pertinent to Matilda's quest or maybe even a way for her to get home. Instead, they were mesmerized by what they saw next.

As Barnaby, Cromeas, Matilda, and Shire watched the water's calm surface, they saw the moving reflection of a young man, about 16 years old, with bright red hair, a milky pale complexion, and freckles covering his entire face. He appeared to be stressed and angry, as if bearing a burden too grave for him to handle.

"That's my poor, dying son, Wiggen!" Barnaby shouted in surprise. "The boy is filled with grief, hatred, and self-pity. He has been ridiculed for being different, and I'm afraid this has stolen his esteem, robbed him of his health, and tarnished his soul."

The three watched with keen interest. Now they witnessed a young Wiggen at age 5. The little boy howled hysterically as two teen-age boys tossed him like a football. Shortly afterwards, alone in a dark cave, Wiggen sobbed like a wounded animal.

"That must be when my boy first decided to believe that there was something inherently wrong with him," Barnaby whispered.

The group looked back to the watery images. A young and apparently angry Wiggen at age 9 stood in a schoolyard. While the other children frolicked and played tag together, Wiggen stood alone with his eyes set upon the ground.

"That poor little boy!" Matilda burst out. "No wonder he's so angry."

The scene now shifted, showing Wiggen at age 12 with his dog, Rudy.

"It's no use, Rudy!" Wiggen fumed. "Nobody likes me. Life is just one big struggle. I know I'm different and guess I'm just unlovable, for some reason. But people are so mean! I'll show them, Rudy. I'll get them. They hate me and I'll hate them right back! Someday, I'll kill them all! And then they'll wish they had treated me better."

"I can see how hatred gains a foothold," shared Cromeas. "I wonder how my own little daughter feels about her lot in life."

"But it gets worse!" Barnaby explained. "Wiggen was recently diagnosed as having brain fog and a hardened heart. The doctors give him only one year at most to live. Since the Earth Change, doctors lost so much technological knowledge, they can't treat ill people effectively."

"Why that's terrible!" cried Matilda. "Is there no hope?"

"None, according to the doctors," Barnaby answered somberly.

"Perhaps it's not too late for Wiggen. Let us maintain hope that he be shown the error of his ways," Matilda pleaded.

The group watched more images in the stream. Wiggen ran down a narrow forest path, carrying some food. As they looked on, they saw Wiggen meet a blind beggar by the side of the trail. While Barnaby, Cromeas, and Matilda watched this scene, a flash of bright light, much like a lightening bolt, shot forth from the stream, striking the three friends. Instantly, they were magically whisked away to that very path where they found themselves suspended as unseen observers, perched high above the action.

The blind man smelled Wiggen's food and implored, "Oh kind sir, would you happen to have a few crumbs to share with a poor blind beggar?"

Wiggen pulled away in disgust saying, "Leave me alone you, old wretch. Go and find your own food! Don't you know I've got troubles of my own?"

With these words, the sky darkened and a deeper shade of gloom covered the scene.

"Look at the sky!" Matilda pleaded, although Wiggen couldn't possibly hear her.

Barnaby and Cromeas noticed the sky instantly change to a darker ominous shade. The air oozed a thick sensation of gloom. Clearly, it was a sign!

Wiggen recoiled in fear, now realizing his error. "What is this sorcery?"

"It is the sorcery of anger turned to hate," the blind man replied. "If you want love, you must be love in the world. If you desire friends, a friend you must be!"

"But no one wants to be *my* friend," Wiggen countered with more than a hint of self-pity.

"I am not saying that life is easy or that the actions of others are always just," the blind man continued. "And I certainly do not condone the hurtful behavior of others. But, surely, have not some kind folk offered *you* an opening, but you refused to be receptive to it? Can every single person be evil at his core? Or, are others just doing the best they know how to in an effort to protect themselves from hurt?"

"I never considered others might be hurting just as much as I am," Wiggen said slowly. "But I *am* different and not worthy of being loved and having the best that life has to offer."

"This is the great lie that you hold as true!" the beggar responded. "Every person has his own gifts and inherent value, and you, son, are no exception. Let us look together at the foolishness of your reasoning: When do you recall first feeling unlovable, not good enough, and unworthy of life's blessings?"

Wiggen put his head down and thought. "I guess it was when I first realized I was different. It was my first day at school. The other kids made fun of me."

"What did they say?" the beggar coaxed.

"They called me little homely freckled boy."

"And what did you decide that must mean?" the old man asked.

"That I was ugly and unlovable and not as good as other people," Wiggen mumbled.

"And is that true?"

"It sure seems to be!" Wiggen sighed. "And then, when I was 8 years old, I stopped growing. Do you know what it's like to be a dwarf?"

"I can't say that I do, but I can guess what you think about it," he replied.

"That's right. I think I'm a freak of nature!" Wiggen whimpered.

"Well, are you open to another interpretation?" the beggar went on.

"I suppose so," replied Wiggen.

"I believe that all people are magnificent and have value. I see our differences as making us special and interesting. Your mind is bright and your soul is kind, deep down. You have sensitivity to the pain of others that will serve you well. In fact, I see your early challenges in life as a huge benefit to you!"

"A benefit? How can that be?" Wiggen asked with a puzzled look.

"Well, I think you'll agree that our world is in pretty tough shape. There is so much pain, hatred, and anger that pollute people's minds and souls that now it darkens the entire sky. You have suffered the pain. You *know* what it feels like to be treated without compassion or respect. You therefore can better empathize with others who might react poorly from their struggles with life's challenges."

"Yes, I suppose I do know why others can be angry," Wiggen agreed.

The old man continued, "What our world is calling for most at this critical time is leadership. And not just angry, self-serving, and vindictive leadership, but the leadership of personal integrity that honors all people and spreads the message of hope, love, and generosity. With the current state of chaos up above and here in Center Earth, think of the many who could use the inspiration of your compassionate leadership! Might you be up to that challenge?"

"But what of my illness?" Wiggen objected. "I will be gone within the year. It's no use. I might as well be dead right now!"

"Do you not know that all illness is an external manifestation of an internal condition?" the old man asked.

"What do you mean?"

"We create our own realities. Be it sickness or health, happiness or sadness, opulence or poverty, fulfillment or resignation."

"You mean to say that *I* created my illness?" Wiggen asked incredulously.

"Yes, I most certainly do!"

"Then how can I be well again?" he asked.

"You must seek the wisdom of one wiser than me for the answer to that question, my lad," the blind man replied.

"I beg your forgiveness, sir, for I now see that what appeared to me as an old blind man is really a clever wizard, sent to gage the lunacy of my befogged mind and the size of my small and hardened heart. I do accept your challenge and, this very day, commit to put aside my own petty concerns. I take on the challenge of learning to be a constructive force and maybe even an inspiration to others. With the empathy I now recognize within, I will aim to give others hope for a better world. I shall commit all my remaining days to this dream of spreading the light of love. And perhaps, as I do so, I shall find the wisdom to which you refer."

The old man smiled and then vanished, as exceedingly wise wizards disguised as beggars often do. But as he vanished, he tossed a parchment scroll toward Wiggen, and it rolled to a stop at Wiggen's feet. Wiggen bent to pick up the scroll and as he did, his father, Cromeas, Matilda, and Shire all appeared before his eyes.

"Is this more sorcery for my benefit, Father?" Wiggen shouted, jumping back in surprise.

"I am learning that our new world, though filled with gloom, is also full of magic and the eternal hope of light, my son. There are magical forces to assist our learning everywhere we go," Barnaby answered. "These are my new friends and partners, Wiggen. Perhaps all this madness *is* for our profit. Read for us this scroll of yours and we shall know more."

Wiggen unrolled the parchment and read:

In times of new like those of old,
When darkness rules and hatred reigns,
Foolish deeds turn warm hearts cold,
And love to hate and joy to pain.
The bliss you seek to warm your souls
Can change your world and all it holds.
To learn these secrets, you must go far,
And seek you the Sage of Shelindar!

As Wiggen finished reading, a map slipped free and floated to the ground. Cromeas picked it up, scanned it quickly, and said, "This map leads to the legendary Throne of Noltis! I've heard tell that high in those mountains lives the Sage of Shelindar. No one knows where he came from or how old he is, but tales go back for ages, so he must be ancient now."

"Where did you learn to read maps, Cromeas?" Matilda asked, quite impressed.

"I studied map-reading and many other skills in military school," he answered matter-of-factly.

"Let us take heed and seek the Sage's wisdom. Perhaps he can heal your afflictions, my boy!" Barnaby encouraged.

"And, perhaps, he can literally shed some light on how to end this state of pervasive gloom," Matilda added. "Perhaps I can learn the secret to restoring the sun's healing light and spread the knowledge throughout the lands here in this world as well as in our world above. The Sage may also be able to help me get back home."

"I think we all could benefit from the Sage's wisdom!" Cromeas added.

Matilda started to roll up the map again, but paused to read an inscription written in gold leaf on the back:

It is never too late to re-invent oneself and inspire others to do the same!

Chapter 5
The Challenge of the Armies

At Barnaby's invitation, the group spent the night at his home nearby. Since they arrived late, after the village slept, no one noticed that Cromeas, a Plabian enemy, was in their midst.

Barnaby informed his wife, Brefta, about the remarkable events that had transpired. She was relieved to have her husband home safe and sound and encouraged by the news of their impending quest to find the Sage of Shelindar. Although fearful at first to have a Plabian cross her threshold, Brefta soon understood the peace that the men had made and warmly welcomed their former foe into their home. She knew that Wiggen's health and future depended upon the miracle they all sought on their journey. After visiting briefly with Cromeas and Matilda, she prepared a wholesome, yet modest meal with the limited provisions she had in store. Matilda noticed that the food seemed more varied and plentiful — certainly no fungi or beetles. They ate, shared stories about their difficult lives since the Earth Change, and dared to dream of a brighter future. All slept soundly, knowing they were among friends, at least for the night.

Matilda and Shire awoke early, eager to get started on their quest. Cromeas, Barnaby, and Wiggen warmly greeted Matilda and Shire at daybreak, when the sky's midnight darkness slowly lightened to a murky grey.

"Good morning to you!" Barnaby smiled. "How are you this day?"

"Well rested, thank you. However, I was thinking some more about the map, and I have a few questions. Tell me about what you know about the lands of Center Earth," Matilda requested.

"Through my discussions with the learned elders here, it appears that the present-day topography of Center Earth is a strange conglomeration. Some ancient lands were already in existence for millenniums in a layer of physical reality closer to the core of the Earth.

The Earth Change altered those lands and combined them with sunken lands from the world above," Barnaby said.

"While some regions were already familiar to us when we fell into this strange new world, many other landmarks were foreign," Cromeas added.

"So I'll probably recognize some places here by recalling my geography studies from the Great Halls of Learning," Matilda reflected.

"Yes, you just might!" Cromeas agreed.

"Tell me what *you* know about the Sage," Matilda continued. "I *know* I never studied about him."

"Legend has it that the Sage lives high in the Enchantment Mountains in the land known as the 'Ends of the Earth.' His lofty stone hall is known to stand carved from the mountainside. It faces the Throne of Noltis, a huge rock formation sculpted into a regal throne. I am told that the Throne is such a grand, towering structure that it can be seen from as far away as the distant reaches of the Slather and the remote sections of the Forbidden Land," Barnaby said.

"Before we begin our journey of enlightenment, perhaps we can start our work right here," Cromeas offered. "Barnaby and I were discussing how much work there is to do right here with our own warring peoples."

"Yes, how can we go off in search of wisdom when so many of our own are filled with anger and hatred toward each other?" Barnaby added. "Last night, before retiring, we sent an urgent request to our respective commanders to assemble their troops for a noon conference upon the Plains of Minites."

"We had better hurry to get there before they all arrive," Matilda said.

And so, Matilda, with Shire ever by her side, accompanied Barnaby, Cromeas, and Wiggen. They reached a bluff overlooking the Plains of Minites with just minutes to spare.

Straining to see through the constant gloom, Matilda looked down upon the plains to see a chilling spectacle. On one side were assembled more than a dozen divisions of Ishite warriors, clothed in full battle garb with silver armor, swords, shields, and spears. The Plabian warriors assembled on the other side in nearly equal numbers. They were bedecked in fearsome black breastplates, with serpentine emblems protruding prominently from their helmets and sharpened axes at the ready by their sides. Quivers filled with poisoned arrows sat upon their backs.

As both armies maneuvered on the field, Barnaby and Cromeas could see that their hasty summons to gather and talk peacefully was being used as an invitation to wage war. With spears and axes in hand and arrows drawn, all stood awaiting the signal from their commanders to begin the battle. Before any horn was sounded, however, the already darkened sky began to boil, and dark clouds dripped a tar-like rain upon the combatants. This thick, black venomous ooze flowed off the warriors, down the field, and across the countryside.

"Here's your first chance to make a difference, Wiggen!" Matilda encouraged.

Wiggen looked at her with a blank stare.

"I'm sorry, it must be the brain fog," he apologized before finally understanding what she meant. "Oh, I get it now!" he answered, seizing this first opportunity to practice leadership. He jumped forward and shouted, "Brave warriors of the Ishites and Plabians, let this day mark a new way for our peoples. Let us put down our weapons and embrace each other as brethren!"

A fierce cry rose up from the field from both sides.

"We have fought to gain our just revenge upon the heathen enemy for more than two millennia, first in the world above and now here. Why, foolish dwarf boy, shall this day be any different?" Harket, the Ishite commander, yelled in reply.

Like the leader he recently declared himself to be, Wiggen did not hesitate. "I, too, have Ishite blood coursing through my veins. I have been schooled in hatred and the need for vengeance, like my great-grandfather before me and his before him. Tell me, brave sir, how has this violence helped our lives? Have our people not suffered enough throughout the course of history?"

Rogin, the Plabian commander, interrupted, "War is the power from which our lives and our death draw energy and meaning. We have been wronged and vengeance shall be ours!"

At these words, a great and angry roar rose up from the Plabian crowd.

"It is either their death or ours!" Harket added. "Why should we care for our enemy when our enemy cares not about us?"

"Because, we all are one!" Matilda shouted.

Against this ominous darkened sky and tar-like rain, a sight never before witnessed in the history of the world unfolded. From above every soldier's head appeared an aura that extended upward. Each aura throbbed with the darkly opaque energy of hate. Within a few moments, the auras from both sides expanded and merged. Like a large and intricate spider web, the auras shared common energy with every other, friend and foe alike, in a connection that showed how all were intertwined.

"What is this sorcery?" demanded Rogin.

Matilda stepped forward. "It is obviously evidence of the links among us all. As you avidly consume the venom of anger and hatred, this poison travels through you to all others, both friend and foe. As you hate others, their hatred grows and returns to poison you. We are all one being with many parts — as a grapevine has many bunches and each bunch, many grapes."

As Matilda spoke, the anger of each warrior, like so much blackened dye, ran forth from the energy emanating from each other man's head, touching and triggering more black energy from others before running back again into the original soldier's body. The angrier the man, the darker the aura about him and the more venom spewed forth to pollute those about him. The more venom that was produced, the more poison was returned to its original owner. At the same time, the clouds continued to grow more menacing, boiling forth their tar-like precipitation in a heavier torrent.

"The opposite is true as well," Matilda continued. "Clean emotions and good thoughts also are spread forth from one to the next. If there is enough that is good, it will flush evil away." But none of the troops seemed to heed her words. Looking for some way to open their minds, Matilda decided she must get closer. She ran down the path onto the plains. As she neared the battle lines, Matilda took the gourd dipper from her belt and dipped up some foul tar from the ground. She then took her flask and poured fresh, clean water slowly into the dipper. At first, there was little change. But as more clean water diluted the dark liquid, what filled the dipper grew clearer and clearer, until at last, all trace of tar was gone.

Throughout the ranks of soldiers, understanding grew. As it did, the darkness clouding their auras grew lighter as well. The more who realized the error of their thinking and abandoned their hatred, the more easily and readily the new healing energy spread to others. Soon, those seeing the light far outnumbered those stuck in their dark ways. Even Rogin and Harket were able to see an end to the old ways of ignorance and intolerance. As more and more grew light at heart, so too did the mid-day sky. A cleansing rain replaced the foul runoff. The ooze dissipated and the land was washed clean. Flowers started to blossom everywhere.

"The sky grows light as does my heart!" Barnaby shouted out. In unison, those upon the plains cheered in agreement.

Matilda stepped closer and laid her hand upon a soldier who was giving thanks for the shift in consciousness. His aura glowed bright and passed from soldier to soldier, brightening the entire company. Soon all glowed in light from the peaceful energy they emitted.

"Won't you spread the news to all you know that anger and hatred need no longer rule your hearts?" Wiggen implored the masses. "Tomorrow we set out to seek the wisdom of the Sage of Shelindar. We welcome any and all who wish to join us in our quest for knowledge and in our thirst for enlightenment!"

That evening, the Ishites and the Plabians celebrated together their mutual commitments to peace and harmony. All shared a feeling of accomplishment not known before in the new world of Center Earth or on the surface above. Although all rejoiced in the newfound hope, none felt more satisfaction than Wiggen, the boy who had feared himself unworthy of contribution and without value.

All slept that night under a newly unfurled banner that read:

"All men are one — Separation is an illusion!"

Chapter 6
True North

The next morning, Matilda, Barnaby, Cromeas, Wiggen, and Shire embarked upon their journey in search of the Sage of Shelindar. They were inspired by the progress made with the warring factions. The events of the prior day gave young Wiggen some hope that others who were just as angry as he had been could recognize the error of their ways, just as he had.

Now his focus turned to finding the Sage in hope that he might offer some advice on how to best deal with his personal afflictions. The Enchantment Mountains were in the far corner of the Ends of the Earth. Barnaby and Cromeas knew that they would need to travel through the perilous, barren terrain of the White Land and the wild country beyond called the Slather. The White Land's desolate desert landscape had once shown an eerie white in the sun — when the sun used to shine in the days before perpetual gloom plagued the land. The white rocks and sand seemed to still hold a feeble glow, but all travelers still needed their torches.

The Slather was the last frontier of civilization, a land generally without laws. It was known as the forest home of ornery outlaws, escaped criminals, and angry varmints who relocated — usually running away from something — from far and wide. Covered by a seemingly endless forest, the Slather was the perfect hideout.

Barnaby and Cromeas appointed themselves to gather some provisions for the long trek ahead. They knew all too well that, at times, food would be hard to come by. Along with two sacks of mushrooms, the two packed a bag of seed cakes that Brefta had baked. Cromeas fitted Shire with a pair of leather water pouches that she gladly bore.

"Wiggen, since you have a compass, I nominate you to lead the way," Barnaby stated.

Wiggen had learned about compasses as a young boy studying under master scouts. Such technology was common in the advanced society existing before the Earth Change.

"I don't want to lead. I have no idea where we'll be going!" Wiggen protested.

"You have the compass. You've carried it with you every day since getting it. Besides, this trek started out as your idea to find the Sage, so you need to lead!" Barnaby insisted.

"Very well," Wiggen reluctantly agreed. He was the only one who ever had owned a compass, so everyone figured he had a reasonably good head start on knowing up from down and east from west. And besides, Shire had a pretty keen nose for danger; so between those two, they all should be just fine.

"The blind man's map says we should follow the Sabre River until it meets with the waterfalls at the Eye of the Icy Gaze," Wiggen observed.

"So now the Sabre River is here!" Matilda exclaimed. "The Sabre used to feed into the sea near my home when I was a little girl. We all figured it was lost in the great upheaval. Now I really feel homesick."

"Many of the geological landmarks from the world above ended up here," Barnaby reminded her.

"I'm sorry for interrupting. We've got much too important work to do for me to feel homesick. Please continue," Matilda encouraged Wiggen.

"The desert land does not begin until after we reach the falls," Wiggen directed. "Shire and I will lead the way. Follow us!"

And so, they were off. For the first few miles, the group skipped along at a merry pace. Shire took her job as a guide seriously. Alhough burdened with the heavy water-pouches, she refused to let them slow her down very much. She would run ahead of the others to make sure the coast was clear and then scurry back with a wag of her tail and an occasional woof to coax the slowpokes along.

They continued on this way for several hours, stopping once to rest and grab a quick snack for just 20 minutes before continuing on the trail again. After another two hours or so on the path, Wiggen began to look concerned. He smacked the compass between his palms. "I think this lousy compass is broken!" he shouted in disgust. "The needle points everywhere but north!"

"Oh, that's just great!" Barnaby scolded. "We've been walking all day, and you just now notice that the compass is off?"

"It's not my fault!" Wiggen shot back defensively. "You're the one who gave me the rotten compass when I was a young child! I didn't want to lead anyway. I knew you'd find fault and put me in the wrong soon enough. Why don't you just lead the group yourself, if you're such a great guide?"

"Now, let's not revert back to our old ways," Cromeas counseled. "We're all in this together! It's no one's fault."

Just then, an old hooded woman appeared, sitting hunched over on the side of the trail. She lifted her head and smiled broadly at the travelers to reveal a nearly toothless grin.

"Where did you come from and who are you?" Wiggen asked with surprise.

"My name is not important. I am a friend who's here to shed some light upon your dilemma," the woman answered calmly. "The compass' accuracy has been distorted by the tremendous amount of negative energy it was exposed to while in Wiggen's pocket all these years. It's actually a great analogy for how most people live their lives," she added. "Let's see if we might turn this challenge into a learning experience. Since we're talking about a compass here, let's see what we know from the Great Halls of Learning about this matter. Matilda, your mother always said that we typically live out our days in the 358 degrees of struggling, suffering, and stepping over the topics that we really need to communicate. That's where all the lies, problems, breakdowns, and mistakes happen. It's where we find ourselves trying but not doing and learning a bit but not *really* getting it."

"How did you know my mother?" Matilda interrupted with a puzzled look.

The old woman just nodded a few more times and smiled again.

"Wait a minute! What are you talking about? You've lost me," Wiggen broke in impatiently.

"Young man, we're talking about your ill health and the costs of your temper and oftentimes nasty attitude!" the toothless woman shot back. "Now I suggest you listen."

"I beg your pardon. I will manage my impatience better. I actually am intrigued by the conversation. So, please say more about the alternative," he asked in a more polite tone.

"The key is to bypass the stories that we tell ourselves and the excuses that get us lost. Instead, we should live our lives following the path that honors our values. That's where our truth lives," the old woman continued. "We usually spend the majority of our time in the 358 degrees of struggle, instead of shifting a couple more degrees, thus keeping on our path in alignment with the truth."

"But *how* do we do that?" Cromeas wondered.

"First, we acknowledge the lie. We admit where we are not being responsible for living our truth."

"But *what* is our truth?" Cromeas went on.

"Our truth is personal to each one of us. One man's truth is not necessarily another's. And our truth always aligns with our most important values."

"So how do we know what those values really are?" Matilda asked.

"Our key values are the essence of our being. They are what make us who we are. They are the ideals we hold most dear."

"You mean like love?" Wiggen asked.

"And like security?" Barnaby added.

"And what about creativity and communication?" Cromeas chimed in.

"Yes, these are all noble values. They are the threads that make up the fabric of our souls — threads that can not be pulled without us becoming very angry, depressed, or non-communicative. So, they *must* be honored. When we honor our values, our lives work. When we violate them, they don't. It's really as simple as that!" the old woman went on.

"So, are you saying that to live our lives on the true path of the heart, it just takes knowing what is most important to us, recognizing when we neglect these values, and taking responsibility for living our truth?" Wiggen said.

"That's exactly what I'm saying, my friend," the wise woman answered. "We can really get to where we want to go in life quickly and without the wasted struggle and suffering if we start to live our most important values. And this starts with identifying where our lives are a *lie*."

"Do you mean our lives are a lie when we feel like we *have* to follow someone else's truth that is not necessarily our own truth?" Matilda asked.

"Yes, those types of values are either imposed upon us by others or we grudgingly accept them as resented obligations. They aren't necessarily our own, but we adopt them out of duty, guilt, or obligation," she answered.

"Like I should keep my room clean, be a good boy, and visit my relatives frequently!" Wiggen added with more than a hint of resentment in his voice.

"But what's wrong with keeping your room clean, being good, and visiting relatives?" Barnaby countered indignantly.

"Nothing is inherently wrong with any of those. In fact, they seem to have great value to many. The problem comes when a person accepts them as an *obligation* or duty and does not truly honor them as true values," the woman replied. "Sometimes it is important to teach a child such values. But the child will reach an age where he must decide to make his own choices about honoring such values. He must decide whether they still serve him or not."

"So, what I hear you're saying is that the bottom line is to make a careful, conscious choice about our behavior. It makes sense that suffering is a useless waste of time," Wiggen said as he pondered these new ideas.

"Yes, suffering is always optional, and responsible behavior dictates that we consciously make choices that empower us, serve our needs, and honor our values," she agreed. "Resignation results when we do not accept this responsibility for making life work optimally. It is the killer of our lifeforce and the reason people stay stuck in lives of quiet desperation."

"I was totally resigned and depressed in my gloomy world above," Matilda shared.

"And I certainly know what that feels like," Wiggen nodded.

"We all do, son," Barnaby consoled. "It seems that, all too often, we settle for less than we deserve because we feel helpless in bringing about change in our lives."

"I now see that that's the lie!" Matilda interjected. "We can always transform our lives by looking at what might be missing to help us honor our key values and move toward our passions. Once we identify where we've blocked our true selves, we simply commit to putting the missing elements in place to break through our challenge."

"And that takes *courage*!" Barnaby shouted, perhaps trying to work up a little more of his own. "I now realize that our entire family has lived in resignation for far too long. We gave up hope that we could affect positive change in our lives. We traded in courage for the relative security of the status quo. We hated the way things were, but we were afraid to do anything. The risk was too scary. And, so we got angry. Later, we succumbed to sadness and despair about why things were the way they were. We could have ended the violence, suffering, and overwhelming numbness in our very souls."

"Great insights!" Matilda laughed and clapped her hands.

"So, we need to remember the choices are ours to make. It's really about accepting responsibility for those choices," Cromeas added.

The old woman agreed, "Yes, if you mean responsibility as an empowering concept, rather than implying guilt, fault, or burden."

She didn't get any further though, because Shire rushed up. The dog had discovered a seed cake wrapper on the ground and brought it back in her mouth.

"Looks like we've been walking around in circles for quite some time, at least since lunch!" Wiggen groaned.

"What's done is done," Matilda consoled. "Anyway, it's getting darker now, so we had better find some cover for the night." Matilda turned to the place where the old woman sat and asked, "Do you know where we might find some shelter, wise woman?" but to the astonishment of all, she was gone!

"Look, there's a cave just ahead," Barnaby yelled, excited at his finding and glad to be able to contribute to the group.

The cave appeared to be dry enough, and it certainly was large enough to accommodate them all.

"This looks like as good a place as any to spend the night," Cromeas sighed, already starting to shift his pack from his shoulders.

The others agreed. As Matilda started gathering kindling for a fire, she found that some past traveler had left a fire ring with charred branches still amid the ashes. She plucked a stick of charcoal from the sooty debris and wrote upon the wall of the cave:

Honor your values, acknowledge the lie, and tell the truth!

Chapter 7
The Cave of Addiction

Gathered around their fire, the travelers sat in the cave, hungry and tired from the day's long trek.

"I can't wait to sleep, but oh, am I hungry," Barnaby complained.

"Look, I have found all sorts of mushrooms growing here!" Cromeas exclaimed. "Let's have our fill before nodding off for the night."

"Good idea," Barnaby agreed.

All four travelers feasted on the tasty treats and were so exhausted from the frustrations of the day that they all fell fast asleep as soon as their heads hit their bed rolls. Shire positioned herself at the mouth of the cave, ready to warn the rest of any impending danger.

Farther back from the high, arched entrance, the cavern's ceiling was decorated with long, cylindrical hanging stalactites. Their many spectacular colors were stolen by the darkness. A hollow and haunting sound of drip...drip...drip echoed throughout the cave, causing Shire to lift an ear and open an eye every so often to reassure herself of its harmless nature. But before long, the constant rhythm playing upon the cavern floor lulled Shire to sleep as well.

The drip...drip...drip of the stalactites upon the floor seemed to grow louder and more insistent, and a murky haze spread through the cave like the cloud arising from adding water to an acid bath. As the dense haze grew, some sound finally roused the four travelers. Barnaby, Cromeas, Wiggen, and Matilda sat up in the blanketing vapors and looked around in alarm.

"What is this evil magic, Father?" Wiggen shouted, his voice trembling with anger and fear. "Are we to be poisoned?"

"I don't know, but I expect we shall soon find out!" Barnaby replied in a tone meant to reassure but clearly laced with fear and frustration.

"I'm sick and tired of these tricks!" Cromeas raged. "Which of you now seeks to deceive us? I demand to know right now!"

"You're the one who found the mushrooms and suggested we eat them!" Barnaby shot back.

"How dare you think this is a ruse perpetrated by one of us?" Matilda lashed back indignantly.

In that moment, moving toward them through the haze, came the old woman who had greeted them on the path. With a soft smile, she spoke, "This is the cave of addiction. You were guided here this night to learn to recognize the destructive emotions that you allow to dictate your moods and deeds. The mushrooms you ate simply triggered your customary reactions of interpreting everything by your own emotional measure. You customarily attribute meanings to the words and deeds of others, meanings that are not factual but based on an addictive emotion. We are all addicted to one. This cave will help you each recognize which one. I invite you now to discover your own personal addictions tonight."

As she spoke these words, she lit a piece of incense and placed it before them in the cavern.

"You have no right to drug us!" Cromeas fumed with anger in his eyes.

"Don't you dare speak to this poor woman in that tone of voice! Don't you know she's trying to help us?" Matilda countered indignantly.

"It's happening all over again!" Barnaby yelled in a frustrated voice. "Why must there always be arguing and struggle everywhere?"

"Now, don't you again add to the problem, Father!" Wiggen pleaded in an angry but fearful voice. "Let them fight among themselves without us getting sucked into the fray."

As the four continued to argue, the old woman simply looked on musingly. "It is now time for the second phase," she instructed in the same gentle tone, and she ignited another cone of incense and tossed it before them.

"Not again!" Cromeas yelled. "Was the first dose not enough? I will not stand for this abuse. I will take my revenge!"

"It's no use!" Matilda replied. "You will always be an angry, vindictive man, looking for the next upset. You are so quick to strike back. I shouldn't even be here. I miss my father and I want to go home!"

"I can't take this fighting. Is there no hope for our people?" Barnaby cried, as he sunk to the floor sobbing miserably, his head in his hands.

"You must be strong, Father!" Wiggen pleaded. "If you cave in, we will lose all hope of finding the Sage of Shelindar. My life is at stake! What will we do?"

With a gentle wave of her hand, the wise woman stopped the troubled conversation. "This display was for your benefit, my friends. Do not be troubled. Let me explain the lesson of the cave." As she spoke, the smoke from the burning incense was gone. Everyone suddenly felt much calmer.

The old woman went on, "Unfortunately, we are all at the mercy of certain emotions that are more addictive than the most potent mushroom or herb. When a situation triggers our reactionary emotions, it is as if we just poisoned our bodies with a toxic potion. For most people, their primary reaction carries a tinge of anger. Someone says something or some event happens, and their anger kicks in. Let us look at what first just happened to each of you."

Cromeas began, "When I feared I was being drugged against my will, I went into a rage. I suppose that is what colors my anger. I rage. I get so upset that I can't see straight, and my first thought is to get revenge."

"And you wonder why you have found yourself constantly at war during your lifetime, Cromeas?" the woman gently queried. "By the way, it was not I who drugged you! You drugged yourself. The incense was harmless. You interpreted it to be a drug. My only role was to expose your all too familiar behavior." She continued. "Actually this is how it always happens. Someone says something or does something. These words or deeds are what actually happened. But then we each interpret the event in our own manner, consistent with the emotional lens we use to see the world. This triggers our most common reactionary emotion, and it gives a certain comforting rush. Yours is obviously raging anger." The woman turned and looked at Matilda. "What did you discover about yourself, Matilda?"

Shaking her head, Matilda responded, "I really should have known better! When Cromeas yelled at you, I became defensive and wanted out of this mess. My thought was 'How dare you talk to an older woman that way?!' My mood is clearly indignant anger. I see it now. It surfaces in almost every conflict I encounter. 'How dare you?!' is my automatic response to every perceived assault."

"Very good insights, Matilda!" the woman smiled. "What about you, Barnaby?"

"Well, my first reaction was frustration. Here we go again, I thought, and this thought made me so angry. I see that I am very easily frustrated. I really must catch myself sooner than I do."

"Thank you, Barnaby. I appreciate your honesty," she acknowledged. "And what did you learn, Wiggen?"

"I saw my anger rise up and immediately turn to fear. It was as if I was being tossed around by those bullies in my childhood, all over again. It made me very mad and afraid at the same time."

"Yes, Wiggen, most of us feel a comforting surge of anger first and then feel a wave of either sadness or fear," the wise woman instructed. "Remember what you felt when I burned the second piece of incense."

"I stayed fiercely angry throughout each mood swing. Rage and fury! I saw black for a few moments," Cromeas confessed.

"Yes, your reaction stays at a high level of furious anger, Cromeas. This is a characteristic of people who commit impulsive acts of violence. By the time they calm down, the damage has usually been done, and regretfully, it's often too late! You must learn to control your rage and give up your need to seek retribution," she somberly warned.

"I saw myself go from indignant anger to sadness," Matilda confessed. "My thoughts typically go from 'How dare you say or do that?' to 'Why would anyone say or do such hurtful things?' and this makes me sad.

I can see how often I construct one-sided explanations that make me indignantly angry first and then terribly sad afterward."

"I do just about the same thing, Matilda!" Barnaby agreed. "The only difference is that I go from frustrated anger to sadness. Even my sadness carries with it a flavor of frustration. I think, 'It's no use!' and so I give up and resign myself to a life that does not work. I can now see it clearly in instance after instance throughout my life."

"And what do you see, Wiggen?" Barnaby asked.

"My anger shifts to fear and also to sadness, just as easily," he replied. "It seems I've been angry, sad, and afraid about literally everything all my life! I suppose it's about time I recognized these patterns and made a new, positive shift."

"That is precisely the secret to shifting out of the destructive emotional pattern!" the wise woman said, sounding proud. "First, ask yourself, 'What specifically happened or what was actually said?' Be exact as though you were reporting only the facts. There's no room for even the slightest negative or distorted interpretation here. It is the story or meaning you place upon the facts that will trigger your emotional mindset."

"But my reaction seems to be automatic," Cromeas interrupted. "I don't have time to stop and separate facts from interpretations. I'm already knee-deep in my addictive emotion by then!"

"Your response is your red flag, Cromeas," she instructed. "When you each can know your most prominent emotions and anticipate them kicking in, you must immediately recognize what is happening. Release your emotion and feel the healing emotion of love. When you let go of your controlling emotion, just relax for a moment and feel love in your heart rather than anger. You can then create a new, truer interpretation about what happened. And that truth will keep your relationships intact."

"You mean, by being open to a new meaning regarding what was said or done, we can release our destructive responses and give the benefit of the doubt to the other person?" Matilda asked.

The woman nodded in affirmation, "Yes, the new meaning we give to what was said or done actually *strengthens* our loving bond with the other person."

"So, instead of interpreting that Cromeas was attacking you, I could have chosen to believe that Cromeas wanted to be loving and peaceful rather than violently angry. For this reason, he protested for all our benefit," Matilda shared.

"That's perfect!" the woman congratulated.

"And I could have seen what happened as an opportunity for learning," Barnaby added. "After all, isn't that true of any challenge?"

"And I could have trusted your wisdom more, Father," Wiggen offered. "I know you always do your best for us."

The woman applauded. "You all have experienced great insights this night regarding how your addictions keep you angry, small, and resigned to a life that is short on joy and love."

"So, then, why would we ever let our emotions dominate us and dictate our reactions to events ever again?" Matilda asked.

"Great question!" the wise woman answered. "Our reactionary mindsets are so addictive because they always make us right and make the other person wrong.

They allow us to feel as though we are dominating in life and not being taken advantage of by others. We may hate being angry, sad, or afraid, but we are so accustomed to these emotions that we often find ourselves going along with them, rather than forcing ourselves to create new meanings that promote love and rapport."

"It seems like we also might be temporarily blinded to what it costs us to act from anger, fear, and sadness." Matilda added.

"Absolutely! We forget that we trade our peace, happiness, partnerships, and love for our need to dominate and feel righteous," the wise woman finished. "You all have made great strides in this cave this night. Congratulations on your courage to learn and your willingness to let go of the beliefs that kept you small."

The wise woman vanished in a flash of blinding light, and when they opened their eyes again, it was to find that it was morning. Rather than sitting upright, they all seemed to have been lying down, as if in a deep sleep. Each looked at the others and knew that they had experienced the same valuable lesson. Was it a dream? They didn't know how it possibly could be real, and yet...

Matilda lit her torch, instantly filling the cave with light. In the light they could suddenly see their proof: They each had, tucked within their belts, a red flag with the words *anger, fear,* or *sadness* written across them.

Matilda unfurled her red flag and wrote upon it, *Recognize, Release, and Re-create!*

She tied the flag to her walking stick as a permanent reminder of the group's commitment to a new way of being. The others did the same before they resumed their journey to Shelindar.

Chapter 8
The Eye of the Icy Gaze

In spite of their tumultuous night, all felt refreshed in mind and body and full of vigor. As always, Shire was the first to announce the arrival of the new day with her three trademark woofs. The group knew by now that she took pride in her daily call to action, and they enjoyed greeting and thanking her for their wake-up call as their first communication with the world.

Now that it was clear to all that the compass was of little use, planning their route was the first order of business.

Wiggen spoke first. "Today, I gladly accept the role of guide for our journey. It's a choice I want to make as a bold step into leadership! Let's study the map that the blind wizard left with us. Perhaps it may shed some light and dispel our confusion."

"Great suggestion, Wiggen," Barnaby beamed. "Perhaps we should have paid more attention to the map from the start. It really is tough to get where you want to go without a detailed map!"

Wiggen carefully unfolded the map. "I see precisely where we went astray yesterday. Instead of staying on the shoreline path paralleling the Sabre River, we took this internal path that goes in a loop. No wonder why we got nowhere fast! If we stay on the course following the Sabre's bank today, it should bring us right to these falls. It may take us about half a day's walk."

"Sounds like a plan!" Cromeas agreed. They all jumped to their feet with Wiggen leading the way.

As Wiggen had predicted, by keeping on the path running along the Sabre River, the group made good and steady progress toward the falls. Shire led the way, and Wiggen and Matilda followed, with Barnaby and Cromeas close behind them. Just as Barnaby and Cromeas had begun to develop an appreciation for each other and the struggles of their respective peoples, so too were Wiggen and Matilda developing the sort of bond that can only arise from listening to what it's like in the other person's world. Each learned more about what was important to the other, but also what was missing that kept life from working smoothly. As they chatted, time seemed to fly.

"I want to thank you for your contribution yesterday as the wise woman shared with us the concept of true north as it applies to our lives," Wiggen begun.

"It was my pleasure, Wiggen," Matilda smiled. "Whenever my mother would speak about it, I always found that topic incredibly interesting; don't you think?"

"More than interesting! It was life-changing!" Wiggen agreed. "What struck me most was the importance of telling the truth."

"Yes, in every area and in every day of our lives!" Matilda said. "It's one of those things that are never handled once and for all. We must resolve each day to speak our truth and take responsibility for everything that shows up around us in our lives."

"I think that's one of the reasons that I became ill," Wiggen confided. "Life was not working. I was not telling the truth, I was not honoring my values, and I was suppressing how I felt. No wonder my body rebelled!"

"When I was a little girl, my mother always talked about the Big Six," Matilda continued.

"What are those?" Wiggen asked curiously.

"The six areas of life where we must tell the truth and admit *the lie* if we are ever to be happy and fulfilled," Matilda said. "These areas are health, wealth, relationships, occupation, recreation, and personal or spiritual development."

"My life was askew in all six! My health was terrible and I couldn't seem to get any better. Because of the war, my parents were unable to work; we had no money and we were always worried about our finances. I had no friends and fought constantly with my family. And with the huge chip on my shoulder, I was not likely to make any new friends anytime soon. I guess you could say my occupation was complaining. Or, maybe that's what I did for fun! I certainly had no hobbies, except for occasionally working with iron. I learned to make all sorts of tools and artistic shapes from the village blacksmith. Looking back on this now, with my terrible attitude, I wonder how he could stand to teach me this skill. Still, I can't remember when the last time was that I had any fun. I was so wrapped up in my self-pity that I didn't even know there was such a thing as personal or spiritual development. My main source of entertainment was to go for long, lonely walks, all the while brooding about my terrible lot in life."

"I'm honored by your honesty. The first step is to recognize what's missing in each area, that if put into place, would make life more fulfilling," Matilda said.

"There have been lots of things missing — having fun, contributing to others rather than just looking at what's in it for me, managing my emotional reactions, giving others the benefit of the doubt, showing love to others instead of contempt. Is that enough for starters?" Wiggen asked sarcastically.

"I'd say it's a great start! My mother also told me who we will be today does not necessarily need to reflect who we were yesterday! The past need not equal the future — if we can change course. We all have the ability to transform our lives if we have the courage to do so. The key is to identify what's missing, make a commitment to a new way of being, and manage that new commitment moment by moment, day in and day out — for the rest of our lives."

"Well, I certainly am willing to do that, Matilda," Wiggen agreed. "What about you and your Big Six?"

"Well," Matilda began, "since the great Earth Change, little has worked for me either. As a young child living by the sea, I had lots of friends. Since the world fell apart, my only friend has been my father. Most of the other villagers trusted no one and kept to themselves, further perpetuating the gloom. These past eight years, I spent most of my time sitting in my cave, going over in my mind, time after time, the lessons I learned in the Great Halls of Learning. I had very little fun, except, of course, when I'd play with Shire. She has really become my best friend and my only source of recreation. If not for her, I'd probably have a hardened heart too!"

Matilda realized too late how critical this must have sounded to Wiggen. "Ah, I mean, you know, I'd be sick too."

"I understand. No offense taken," Wiggen assured her.

"Thanks to my mother, I feel like my life lately has been guided by a personal development focus. For this I am so grateful!" Matilda continued. "As far as the other aspects are concerned, I do have a commitment to see that all areas of my life are fulfilling and balanced. That is, after this quest is complete and I can return home."

The group soon found themselves at the end of the path, overlooking the falls. Suspended above the spraying flume, the sky here was considerably lighter and less gloomy. The jumping spray from the cascade danced upon their faces, providing a bit of refreshing relief from their dusty journey.

As the four looked upon this spectacle in awe, they heard melodious voices sing out:

Welcome to the falls of the Icy Gaze,
Dear companions we've yet to meet.
Come dine and drink and share your tales,
Your friends are waiting to greet!

As the song finished, hundreds of elves appeared suddenly out of the mist.

Stepping forward was a tall, lean elf with blond, flowing hair that fell softly upon his shoulders. "We are the elves of the falls, and I am Nimi, at your service, dear friends."

"We are travelers from the Iopu Valley and other lands. It is our pleasure to meet you," replied Barnaby, grateful for the hospitality. "We journey to the Enchantment Mountains in search of the Sage of Shelindar."

"So, you are seekers of wisdom?" Nimi asked.

"We are indeed, Sir Nimi. You have likely heard of our conflicts. We come from a people who share our need for enlightenment. Terrible wars and greed have exacted their toll on our peoples and our future is in great jeopardy. You shall find us receptive of any wisdom you might choose to offer," Cromeas added.

"Come then and first feast with us, hear our tales, and share with us the happenings of your world," Nimi invited.

The elves were, indeed, wonderful hosts. They sang songs celebrating life and love, shared delicacies from hidden nooks and valleys in the White Land, and drank the finest of elfish ale. The gloom that had been so pervasive elsewhere was not nearly so bad here. As a result, food was more plentiful and found in greater variety than elsewhere in the lands.

After all had eaten and drunk to their hearts' content, Nimi spoke, "Tell us of your struggles and of your dreams."

"Where should we begin?" Barnaby responded with a sigh. "Our world is in chaos. Our peoples have known only warfare and hatred. There is famine, poverty, and suffering throughout our lands. We humans who landed here in Center Earth struggle with the horrible effects upon our children. The Earth Change has stunted the growth of our children. My own son is but one example of this horrible change, and it is told that there are other, far worse, repercussions taking place throughout the lands."

"Long before the recent Earth Change, a prior cataclysm occurring eons ago formed this place we now call Center Earth. Those changes also created us elves. But we are grateful for the creation of our race and hold ourselves in high esteem. I see no reason why you might not hold your dwarf children with an equally high regard," Nimi offered. "All beings have value, no matter their differences. It is how you perceive them that counts. We treasure our peoples' differences."

"I never considered looking at it that way," Cromeas replied. "It certainly would make quite an impact upon their self-esteem if others did not view them as inferior."

Wiggen sat silently listening to this exchange before he finally spoke. "Thank you, Nimi, for sharing that wisdom. As one who has suffered the burden of discrimination, I can attest to the harm these perceptions of others cause toward my kind. I know deep inside that I am intelligent, magnificent, and loving. I also know that I am worthy of being loved and having the best that life can offer. As one who is different, I can appreciate the pain of those who are ostracized."

"What, then, will you do with this insight, Wiggen?" Nimi asked.

Wiggen sat back and thought quietly for a few moments. The others could practically see the fog lifting from his mind. "Why, I shall teach the world that all beings are equally worthy of respect, love, and the chance to make the most of their lives. I shall lead by example, foregoing hatred while embracing diversity. I shall answer aggression with love and teach others that love can soften the hardened hearts of men and heal our troubled planet, here in the lands of Center Earth and above on the surface. I shall be an inspiration of what is possible to myself first and then to others. And when I weaken and revert back to that which is merely convenient in the moment, I shall return myself to this commitment and ask others to likewise hold me accountable to this pledge." Wiggen spoke these words with a tear in his eye — very uncharacteristic for those suffering from hardened heart syndrome!

"Words of an inspirational leader if I have ever heard one," Nimi applauded. "Let us invite you, our friends, to join us in a tour below these falls." As he spoke, Nimi stood and waved his arm in a gesture encouraging all to follow him.

Barnaby and Cromeas jumped to their feet first. Matilda reached for Wiggen's hand and they both led Shire in the procession behind their new friend.

They passed through an area of the falls midway to the base. Nimi motioned for them to stop and look forward. With eyes wide open, they watched a series of scenes unfold before their vision.

Here's what they saw: The land was rich and lush. Prosperity and peace were hallmarks of this world. Man, dwarf, elf, and other beings lived in harmony with each other in scene after scene. Each person contributed to the next. The world was bright with light and the sky radiated an uplifting blue hue. The warmth of the sun shone on all living creatures and all types of vegetation flourished. The visitors felt the peace that comes from a happy heart and a loving soul, as they watched what they hoped was the future scenario for the world.

As they neared the base of the falls, Nimi signaled for the visitors to follow him. At the wave of his hand, Cromeas, Barnaby, Matilda, and Wiggen stepped single file behind him, matching him step for step. As if in a trance, they walked through what Nimi called the Eye of the Icy Gaze. It appeared to be a great rock that resembled an eye whose gaze never wavered. The group marched into the cascading water and out the other side of the falling spray.

Before them, against the backdrop of the mist, was the projection of a scene. The visitors recognized themselves as the players, as if upon a stage. The sky was again dark and foreboding. Barnaby and Cromeas recognized themselves as warriors in the heat of a fierce battle. Each was tallying the number of enemy soldiers he had killed or maimed that day. As the scene shifted, it became clear that they were battling not just each other's people but the dwarf race as well. They saw Wiggen lead a charge of their enemies' armies against his father and his friend. They were surrounded in what was obviously a fierce battle between the world of men and all the other races. All who saw knew there was no joy or satisfaction in this work.

The scene continued. Matilda saw herself as a weak and helpless widow, living in filth, poverty, and ignorance. She was clearly helpless and unable to stem the tide of hate and suffering. Her state of resignation had returned in full force. She resembled one barely living in the world with a soul that had long ago gone numb.

Nimi spoke, "You have just passed through the Eye of the Icy Gaze, separating the positive from the negative dimensions of your characters. Everyone has this front, positive side and a back, dark side of their being. It is your choice as to which of the two you will embrace. What you are witnessing is the materialization of each of your greatest fears."

"But which is real and which imagined?" Wiggen asked — his mind still gripped in fear from the reality of the spectacle.

"Both are very real. The Eye merely shows some of the probable realities that may result from your fears being turning into actuality. An infinite number of possible realities can unfold depending upon whether the front or back sides of your being are embraced. One reality will follow and take shape from the choices you and others make. Each choice uncovers yet another choice. Doing nothing is also a choice. If you do nothing, the horror of the world you have witnessed will continue to evolve. You will simply play no part in preventing the calamity. It is the path your world is already set upon. Men will follow their lesser emotions and the result is clear. War, hatred, suffering, and darkness will result," Nimi replied somberly.

"And what about the other, more positive possible world? What will that outcome need to exist?" Barnaby asked.

"Leadership with integrity. Doing the right thing and not counting the cost. Someone must initiate either one outcome or the other. If it be not you four, I fear, the balance shall tip toward darkness. We all possess both light and darkness in our souls. It is our choices that determine the fate of our world and the path that our lives will follow. One is as likely as the other. It all rests upon your decision to lead courageously, be resigned to allow others to dictate the choices, or worse yet, to follow your moods of hatred, sadness, and fear and take the vengeful path that these moods dictate. Your actions, aligned with your commitments, will indicate what choices you make daily, with love or hate, courage or cowardice. Either your greatest fears or your greatest hopes can be realized. It is your daily thoughts and beliefs that will get translated into reality. Choose wisely."

With these words, Nimi disappeared. With him went the scenes and all traces of the night's festivities. In its place, a rainbow appeared along with the words:

Will you honor your commitments and take the path of heart?

Or will you do what is convenient? The choice is yours!

Exhausted from what they had witnessed, the group silently made their way to shore and fell asleep, only to experience an uneasy night filled with fitful dreams.

Chapter 9
The Completion Chamber

The next day actually began for the friends hours before the time when dawn should have been, had there been a sun to be seen rising upon the horizon. None of the travelers slept more than a few minutes at a time the night before, so they agreed to replace their tossing and turning with a return to action and get an early start on the next day. Cromeas and Barnaby returned to the river above the falls in order to fill their water sacks. They were about to enter the White Land and they knew from the tales that water was scarce in this desert.

"I don't know about you," Cromeas spoke, "but I'm scared. I feel I just *have to* manage my dark side and the terrible anger I still feel from time to time. Trouble is, I fear I'm too lazy to keep my evil side under control. I don't even know what I need to do to fulfill the future I truly want."

"Sounds like you are attached to the outcome you want," Barnaby offered. "I agree that there's just too much at stake to take our potential lightly. But when a person is attached to an outcome, there is little room to act powerfully. You'll constantly worry about if you are making a mistake. You'll be second guessing every action. I know about this because our commander, Harket, spoke to us about how this can limit our power and effectiveness in dealing with others."

"So what's the option then?" Cromeas asked.

Barnaby replied, "I think it's simply resolving to act from our commitments, moment by moment, no matter what challenges we may face. I'm personally totally committed to managing my own dark side from this point forward. At the same time, I know that I'll have my weak moments and make some mistakes. After all, perfection is not attainable, but excellence is. My commitment is to recognize the opportunity to take action and then act boldly, in a way that honors my values."

"So, you're saying that it's not enough to decide now to act from our values?" Cromeas asked.

"As I see it, that's just the first step. To be successful, we must resolve each day, maybe minute by minute, to manage our commitments powerfully. It's not a one-time resolution since this one is an ongoing lifelong commitment."

Meanwhile, back at the camp, Matilda and Wiggen were having a similar conversation.

"After last night's insights, I've *really* decided to step into leadership and into my power!" Wiggen told her. "The alternative is just too scary! I now see that finding the Sage of Shelindar means much more than just discovering the secret to my own health and well-being."

"Yes, the fate of the entire world depends upon our success," Matilda agreed.

"It's a lot easier for me to focus upon contributing to others than just pursuing my own selfish needs and agenda!" Wiggen added.

Just then, Cromeas and Barnaby made their way into camp. Shire jumped and frolicked around their legs as if to say "What took you so long?"

"Let's get underway!" Wiggen said. "Follow me. I've been studying the map and see the way we must go is through the desert of the White Land."

The group climbed up the cliff and followed in the direction that Wiggen and Shire led. Before long, the trees and vegetation gave way to a rocky and barren landscape. In another mile, the rocks were gone and all that could be seen ahead was the desolate sweep of white desert sands.

"We must stay close together as we pass through the desert," Barnaby instructed. "I hear that sandstorms can block one's vision in all directions."

"And who knows what creatures may lie in wait for unsuspecting prey!" Wiggen finished.

At that moment, as if Barnaby had predicted the future, a gust of wind, stronger than any gust any of them had ever experienced in their lives, swept over their path, covering them from head to toe in sand. This swirl of sand was all-enveloping. It shut out all light and sound. They each had the eerie sensation of being totally alone, cut off from all human touch and from every one of their own senses. The envelope of total quiet, total darkness, and total lack of tactile sensation made Cromeas fear he would soon go crazy.

Matilda's first thought was for Shire's safety and that of her comrades. But on the heels of that thought, she heard a silken voice in her head say, "Fear not, Matilda, for all are well."

Matilda thought, "My mind must be playing tricks on me."

The same voice replied, "You have entered the completion chamber; be not afraid."

Matilda opened her mouth to speak but found no voice available. Instead, she heard herself think her next question, "What do you mean by a completion chamber?"

The silky voice told her, "In this space between physical realities, you will encounter those with whom you have unresolved communication issues. These are the people with whom you are still incomplete."

"What do you mean by incomplete?" Matilda thought.

The voice replied, "You are incomplete with anyone you are still angry with, anyone you have wronged or been wronged by, anyone to whom you have words left unspoken. This is your opportunity to complete the past and stop wasting the energy you spend thinking about these unresolved issues. When a person is not complete, she must spend precious energy stuck in the past. If you are to be powerful in the present, these issues must be resolved. Let the process begin!"

Matilda found herself envisioning her father's face. Costas looked so vivid in her mind that before she knew it, Matilda found herself speaking to him. "Father, I've missed you so much since landing here in Center Earth."

She felt no surprise that Costas should reply. "I've missed you too; but know, my daughter, that my spirit is with you always, just as your beloved mother's is."

"Father, I am worried about your sadness since the great Earth Change. I see how resigned to the daily struggle of life you have become."

"It is true. I long for my old life by the sea with you and your mother. My days have become stagnant."

"But this need not be!" Matilda said with spirit. "You have much to live for and much to contribute to others. Those in the village are scared and confused like you. They need you to rise up out from your stagnation and lead them. Inspire them to resume living a full life once again. You and they can not do this in isolation."

"But, how can a simple fisherman like me lead others when I have great difficulty leading myself?" he pleaded.

"It's about believing in yourself, Father. You must risk and have the courage to snap them out of the rut that we all were in for too many long years. Don't dwell on the shame and sorrow in your heart but look at the good you can do for your fellow villagers." Matilda finished, "This was my incompletion. I have said what I needed to. I am now complete. Thank you for listening. I miss you and I love you!"

Her image of Costas vanished from her mind before he could reply, but she knew she didn't need his words. Her need had been to speak the truths that she had held back for so long. And, somehow, she felt sure that the real Costas back on the surface had indeed heard her.

Cocooned in the silence of the sand storm, Wiggen heard a husky voice in his head that offered, "This is now your chance to complete your past."

He no sooner decided to accept the challenge than he had to rub his eyes in disbelief. Appearing before him were the bullies who had tossed him about playfully as a young boy. Wiggen looked the boys straight in the eye: "Why did you treat me so cruelly when I was so young and impressionable? I chose to think I was not loveable and was unworthy of all the good things in life because you showed no concern for my feelings. I have been angry at your callousness ever since. I still bear this pain."

The two boys replied, "Please forgive us. We did not realize the hurt we caused you. We, ourselves, felt inadequate, and tossing you about made us feel powerful. We meant no harm. We are so sorry."

"Thank you for your apology. I forgive you. Go in peace!" Wiggen wished them.

Immediately the two boys disappeared and Wiggen's mother appeared before him in their place. He immediately knew what he had to say to her.

"Mother, why did you not protect me from harm as a young child? Did you not see the pain and turmoil I faced in fight after fight? Could you not have counseled me better? Did you not love me enough to teach me the ways to survive and thrive in this new world?"

Tearfully, Brefta looked at her son. "My beloved boy, I love you more than I love life itself! Please forgive me my faults and weaknesses. I did the best I knew how, which I see was not nearly good enough. I was overwhelmed in dealing with a new and harsh land torn apart by war and a son afflicted with the burdens of being different and not fitting in. I went numb out of my inability to cope with the challenges that life had dealt me. I love you. Please forgive me."

Wiggen smiled and the weight of years of anger was instantly lifted from his brow. "Thank you, Mother, I now understand. I love you and forgive you. I know you did your best. You actually contributed to my understanding and the development of my empathy for others out of the pain that I have experienced. So, I see that it was all for the good, all meant to be." With these words, her image was gone.

Dozens of others appeared to take their turn at completion, for Wiggen had led a troubled and angry life. With some, Wiggen asked questions or probed for clarity: Why had they said or done the things that had hurt him? With others, he merely said what was in his heart without needing to hear a reply. Just saying what was on his mind was enough in many cases for him to reach completion. In the end, Wiggen felt squeezed flat — exhausted and yet very satisfied. Nothing more remained unsaid. Years of pain were unleashed from his soul.

Barnaby and Cromeas, as former warriors, had wronged many and been wronged by many more in return. Still, most of their encounters ended with forgiveness and expressions of love. As the four finished with their completions, the sandstorm subsided and the calm after the storm was restored. Even the sky appeared lighter, just like our friends' spirits.

"Wasn't that the best storm you've ever survived?" Barnaby asked the group.

"I feel 10 years younger and 50 pounds lighter!" Cromeas replied.

"We all do," Matilda agreed.

"Communicating all that I had bottled up inside me all these years felt so good!" Wiggen exclaimed. "I now realize that most everyone I was upset with did the best they knew how to do. They were struggling with their own demons as much, if not more so than I was. It felt so good just to get all those feelings off my chest."

Cromeas agreed. "When I put myself in the other person's shoes, I could easily understand why they acted as they did. Not only did I create empathy for them, but I also felt their pain and understood their struggle. It was then so much easier to love them and forgive them. I wish everyone could experience completion of their troubling past!"

The rest of the day, the group skipped along in their journey through the remaining desert lands with the sort of ease that would have had others think they were skating along a smooth lake of ice instead of walking through a barren and challenging desert. With Shire leading the way, that night they reached the border of the White Land and made camp in preparation for the next day's adventure into the Slather. Matilda lit a lantern with her torch and hung it high to illuminate the camp. The lantern's glow struck a banner that Wiggen made in honor of their new understandings. It read:

> *Empathy is the key to forgiveness.*
> *Forgiveness is the path to love.*
> *Love is the key to peace and harmony.*

All slept soundly, as though they were at home in a familiar bed instead of camped between an unforgiving desert and an untamed wilderness.

Chapter 10
The Slather

The morning came, as gray as ever. Despite their renewed feelings of hope and anticipation from the night before, the companions sensed that the air was filled with apprehension. Everyone in Center Earth had heard the wild, almost unbelievable tales about the jungles of the Slather. Even the gloom in the sky above, pervasive since the upheaval, had only a slight effect on the denseness of the area's vegetation. The place was legendary, but for all the wrong reasons. It was reportedly the hideout of many a renegade, goblin, and outlaw.

This morning, Shire was much more agitated than usual. As the group proceeded down the narrow jungle trail that led through the Slather's dense vegetation, she paced nervously up and back, ever vigilant. As they advanced, she spotted a python overhead, curled on a tree branch ready to strangle Wiggen. She let out a warning woof just in time.

The group made slow progress for a few more hours in this fashion. Every twig snapping or rustle from the trees was a signal of possible peril ahead. If not for Shire's keen senses and alertness to danger, the group surely would have suffered any number of predator attacks as they advanced their way forward closer to their destination.

"My nerves are on edge!" Barnaby remarked after traversing several miles in this fashion. "How much longer do we need to go before we exit this jungle?"

Wiggen studied his map seriously before responding, "It looks like about another two hours journey before we reach the closest border of the Ends of the Earth."

With no warning, a woven net shot out from a camouflaged hole in the ground, immediately ensnaring them all. A sticky white substance coating the net had the four travelers and Shire stuck to the sides like glue.

"What is this treachery?" Wiggen shouted.

In reply, they heard a song that sent shivers down their spines:

When spies come calling
In lands so brash,
Our nets go hauling
In cargos of trash.

"Why, we're not spies!" Matilda yelled indignantly. "We are emissaries on a mission of peace and light."

"And we're certainly not trash!" Barnaby countered.

The reply came back:

We trust not the lies
From tongues of spies.
For invading our space
You will pay with your lives.

Matilda had wound up in the net on the top side of the pile. As she looked out through the mesh, she saw many gleaming pairs of eyes staring back at her from behind every tree.

"Who are you?" she screamed, more terrified than she ever thought possible. She tried to calm her terror by breathing slowly and deeply, something her mother had once shown her.

Once again, mocking voices replied:

We are the righteous,
Oppress us no longer.
Vengeance is ours,
Your treachery makes us grow stronger!

"You have it wrong! Our way is righteous. You are the treacherous ones!" Wiggen yelled furiously, and he struggled even harder against the sticky ropes.

And back came the response:

Be quiet and refrain!
Your lies are in vain,
For your flesh will soon rot
Inside our stew pot!
And word will then travel,
From every village and steeple,
Of how dangers unravel
For all who mess with our people!

Within the net, the friends were now in a panic. "I can't believe we came this far only to die at the hands of these villains!" Barnaby cried. "It's just not fair!"

"Life isn't fair," Cromeas consoled him morosely.

"Let's not panic!" Wiggen said.

"Yes, we have too much to accomplish to give up this easily!" Matilda agreed. "What about the contributions we have yet to make in this world? What about our life purposes and the gifts we still must share with others?"

The plucky girl kept looking for an escape even as she was speaking. Just then, Matilda had an idea. She leaned as close to Shire as the gummy glue would allow and whispered, "Shire, do you think you can chew a hole through this net?"

Giving an agreeable woof, the dog stretched her neck to reach the ropes and started to gnaw. Shire made a small hole in the net, as the others tried to wedge it wider. Their captors noticed and came rushing over to foil their feeble efforts.

"Go, Shire, run and save yourself!" Matilda screamed.

Shire wiggled free, sprang from the net, and ran off into the jungle. The goblins tried to give chase, but they were no match against her speed and determination. Within seconds, she was out of sight and out of their reach.

"Well, at least Shire got away," Wiggen muttered, feeling only a little consoled. He was stuck like a bug. Some leader he had turned out to be! He tried not to imagine what his father and the others must think.

"That may be so, but you will not be so fortunate!" Karbon, the goblin leader, cursed back. "Tomorrow at dawn, you shall get your wish and serve as a contribution — to our breakfast!"

As evening came, the goblins doubled the number of guards posted around the travelers. Things certainly looked as dark as the starless night sky above their heads and the cast iron pot beneath their net.

"How are we going to get out of here?" Cromeas whispered.

"I have no idea," Barnaby sighed.

"It really does look hopeless," Wiggen said with the resignation that had marked his earlier days.

"Is there some way that we could take our minds off of our predicament for a while?" Matilda asked. "I've always found that when things look bleakest, it often helps to think of something else, even if for a little bit." She wanted to feel Shire's warmth and see her father's smile. "Maybe we could talk about something."

"I'm all for that," Wiggen agreed. "But what shall we talk about?"

"Well, for starters, I do not know what your life purposes are. I actually don't know what any of you see for your life's work," she began.

"It seems ironic to be speaking of our life purposes now when we have only a few hours left before we become soup!" Barnaby commented sourly.

"Let's pretend that we have the next 300 years ahead of us to live boldly and with passion. What could each of you do that might make each day worth arising out of bed with energy and gusto?" Matilda went on, recalling a similar conversation her mother had had with her not long ago.

"I'm not sure," Cromeas considered.

"Well, Cromeas, what qualities were you known for as a child?" Matilda asked.

"You mean those qualities I gave up on long ago?"

"Yes, before the dry rot of resignation took hold in your life," she coaxed.

"Well, as a young child, I was known as the class clown. I was always joking and having fun and thinking about how I could make others laugh," Cromeas reminisced.

"What happened to that side of you?" Barnaby exclaimed in surprise.

"I guess that I just lost the spontaneity in my approach to life and the funny little kid inside me died."

"He didn't die, Cromeas! I bet he's still there, waiting to come out and play!" Matilda encouraged.

"Well, in the unlikely event that we ever get out of this mess, I would be so excited to live every single day communicating and having fun. Actually, I'd love to communicate to others about how to have fun while helping them do so!" Cromeas stated with great satisfaction.

"So, your life purpose is to *be* fun!" Matilda managed a smile.

"Yes, it is!" Cromeas shot back with a grinning, cross-eyed look that made everyone laugh. "That really feels great to make you laugh! What about you, Barnaby, what's *your* life purpose?"

Barnaby furrowed his brow in confusion. "I'm not sure."

"Well, what qualities were you known for as a kid?" Cromeas prodded.

"I really wasn't known for much. I was always the quiet kid standing alone in the courtyard while everyone else played." Barnaby went back to that moment in his mind, and a wave of sadness overwhelmed him.

Matilda continued, pretending not to notice. "What would give you the most satisfaction?"

After a few moments to compose himself, he said, "I would be a friend to those in need of one. That would be something worth living every day for the next *3000* years!"

"That's one amazing life purpose, Barnaby!" Cromeas swallowed hard before he spoke again. "You make a wonderful friend and I'm honored that you're mine!"

Barnaby turned to Wiggen. "What about you, my son? What's your life purpose?"

"You mean if I were not dying of a hardened heart and brain fog?" Wiggen replied, but without any true bitterness. "It would be to serve as an example of love in the world and to inspire myself and others that anyone can accomplish anything if they believe they can! After being so angry and resigned for so long, it's high time I started living my life purpose, even if it's only for a few paltry hours. I know too well what it's like to give up on life, so I would really be a champion in support of others to live boldly and with passion."

"Well said, Wiggen!" Matilda told him. "I can say that truly you are already an inspiration."

"Your praise means much, because you're one who has helped me learn that life is not all about me," he replied. "If I weren't in this net, I would seek for ways to contribute to others. But what about you, Matilda? What is your life purpose?" As Wiggen waited for her answer, he wondered if she had always looked so full of light. Or was he just now paying attention? Either way, Matilda glowed from within, beating back the darkness around them.

She said, "My life purpose is to vanquish the gloom and light the way for others. It is to spread the message of light and love to all corners of the world. And that includes even here!"

Wiggen thought Barnaby and Cromeas were noticing her new incandescence, but they kept silent. Matilda seemed oblivious. "There is no greater need, Matilda," Wiggen concurred. "That is clearly your gift to the world."

"Yes, but it is nearly daybreak and there is no sign of hope in sight. How are we ever to escape these goblins?" she wondered, and the eerily wonderful glow began to dim. But before their spirits sank completely, they heard some ruckus from the edge of the encampment.

The travelers looked out from their woven prison to see Shire racing toward them like a jackrabbit and Nimi on horseback by her side with an army of elves just behind.

"We knew you must be in danger when Shire appeared in our camp. She was frantic and out of breath, tugging our clothes to make us follow her," Nimi said.

He dismounted and shouted, "You, who have bound our friends, show yourselves now! State your reasons for this aggression."

Karbon, the goblin leader, stepped out from behind the tree where he had hidden. "These spies have trespassed upon our lands, with evil intent, no doubt. We were only defending ourselves and sending a warning signal to others with similar ill intentions."

"I can vouch for the good intentions of these travelers," Nimi replied. "Their mission is to spread the light of love, peace, and understanding to all men. They are not spies!"

"How can we know you speak the truth?" Karbon questioned. "We have heard such talk before, only to have the spies bring back forces to wipe out our people. We have learned it is wiser to kill than to be killed!"

Matilda spoke, "You speak the old tongues of fear, hatred, and retribution. This will only lead to more suffering and pain. Our mission is to speak a new message of hope. We want to live in peace, side by side, with those of all cultures and backgrounds. It is time we put aside our weapons and together find another means of resolving our differences!"

Wiggen continued, "We, too, have known great suffering, fear, and mistrust born of hatred. If we always do what we've always done, we will always have what we've always had! Are you content to have your families die so that you must seek vengeance in return? Will this bloody cycle never end? Is it not time for a new way? We journey to where the Sage of Shelindar lives. He surely will share his wisdom, so that we might learn the secrets to living with all others in peace. I implore that you allow us to pass through your lands. Once we complete that part of our mission, we promise to return and share the Sage's wisdom with you. Please trust us so that we might prove worthy of your trust."

Karbon hesitated in thought for a moment before speaking. "We have tried the ways of peace before in vain. They have brought us deception and suffering. Others seek to oppress us and keep us in poverty. My people have learned that the only way to ward off aggressors is to put the fear of our righteous retribution in their souls. It is through inspiring this terror that we have survived. Without it, we would surely have perished at the hands of our enemies."

"I know this has been your experience and now understand why you do not trust, but if we were ones who meant harm, wouldn't these elves have finished with you already? You wouldn't be standing and talking. Let this day make the start of a new possibility. Let us support you as your allies in a mutual quest for peace and harmony in every land," Matilda said.

Nimi spoke, "We, too, shall champion this noble cause. Please take this chance offered today to try a new way. Join us in our mission."

The goblin commander stepped back behind a tree to confer with his generals. He emerged and signaled for his men to release the prisoners from their net. With hands formally outstretched in friendship, he spoke, "We accept your proposal. Let us join with your hands and hearts today to make a new way for the sake of all our children and all their children."

And so, that evening, a new bond was begun between the different factions representing the races of goblins, elves, dwarves, and men. In place of traveler stew, the parties feasted upon the many delicacies and fine ales for which the Slather became known from that day forward. Several goblin generals melted their black swords, and Wiggen forged a lantern. He hung it upon a great tree. Matilda and Wiggen, together with Barnaby, Cromeas, Nimi, and Karbon led a procession in which each person helped light the lantern, beginning a tradition all hoped would continue to ignite hope and the more noble emotions of love and harmony, long ago cast aside in favor of war and hatred.

The travelers shared their newly declared life purposes with the others and encouraged them to declare *their* own gifts and purposes. After a rewarding evening of building friendships and sharing dreams of new possibilities, they went to bed, satisfied that a new possibility had taken root that day.

Chapter 11
The Vision Pool

The next morning, the four friends, awakened as always by Shire's barks, got off to an early start, each one eager to begin living their newly discovered life purposes. They knew from Wiggen's map that only about half a day's journey through the jungle remained before they would reach the land known as the Ends of the Earth.

As they made their way through the jungle, they savored a newfound sense of joy — the vibrant joy that comes from living beyond one's life expectancy. All knew that yesterday could have been their last day. So, today seemed to all of them like a holiday gift they had suddenly received as a surprise. The conversation that morning was around how each would manifest his or her life purpose in the world.

Barnaby said, "I feel like I have a new lease on life! Last night I did my best to extend a hand of friendship to the goblins. I understand better now why they committed all those horrible atrocities in the past."

Cromeas continued, "I just want us to have as much fun as we can today — and every day. After all, my life purpose is inspire people to have fun! Matilda and Wiggen, do you think while spreading your message of light and love, you might need to have a bit of fun here and there, too?"

"Absolutely!" Wiggen shot back. "We can never get too much fun in our days."

"So, perhaps we can use our time here, journeying together, to better craft our visions for the rest of our lives," Matilda challenged.

"How do we do that?" Barnaby asked curiously.

"By envisioning what every single aspect of our lives will be like when all our key values are being honored and we're living our life purposes," she explained. "Like where will you live and with whom? How will you spend a typical day at work and a typical one at play?

Or maybe, will these be the same, since you'll be living boldly and with passion? What will you surround yourself with materially and spiritually and who will be your friends and playmates? And, of course, who will you contribute to as you live out your days? Any worthwhile vision must have elements of contribution to it. It if is only self-serving, it will inspire no one to join you in its fulfillment or in creating visions of their own!"

The group's direction shifted abruptly as the path they were following turned sharply to the east.

"What is *your* vision, Matilda?" Wiggen asked.

As Matilda opened her mouth to begin speaking, just steps before her, Barnaby and Cromeas stopped unexpectedly on the trail. The men's eyes and mouths were both open wide. An eerily beautiful jade green pond stood before them. Its surface glistened and reflected the surrounding mountains. The tranquility reminded Matilda of the sea back home, before the Earth Change, on those rare summer nights when a full moon cast its mesmerizing magic upon the water. As all four stared intently at the motionless reflection before them, all of a sudden, a series of scenes proceeded to unfold, suspended for all to see, just above the water. Fascinated, the group saw themselves standing in a circle, holding hands, and raising their four torches up high. As they bowed their heads in unison, they were suddenly surrounded by their families. Costas, Kuchina, Brefta, and a band of other family members surrounded the four travelers. They too held torches of their own, but the torches weren't lit. As they bowed in what seemed to be reverence to their actions, their torches were lit by those that Matilda, Wiggen, Barnaby, and Cromeas held. Beyond this second ring stood a third ring of people and then a fourth, and then an infinite ripple of rings of people. The people appeared to go on into infinity. In a rhythmical and almost effortless procession, the fire from each torch ignited each subsequent row of torches held high by the next group of people. Suddenly, the gloominess of the day gave way to an endless number of brilliant torches that illuminated the sky and the land beneath it.

The visionary reflection shimmered for a moment and then vanished. The brilliant glow of light faded into darkness again, and the four friends knew they witnessed the ultimate manifestation of Matilda's vision. The men knew their visions could become real, too. But they wouldn't see any more visionary reflections — the jade green pond was no more. In its place, a scroll lay on the grass before them. Matilda reached for the parchment, unrolled it, and read aloud:

When darkness reigns o'er all the land,
And hatred raises its dreaded hand,
Four now come to end the pall
And bring their light to one and all.

As the group looked up, they saw the great red rock formations of the Enchantment Mountains with the Throne of Noltis prominently visible in the distance. They knew from legend that the immense kingly hall carved out of the mountainside lay just behind it. Instinctively, they just knew it would not be long now before they would meet the legendary Sage of Shelindar.

Chapter 12
The Throne of Noltis

With eager anticipation, the group forged ahead. Shire once again led the way, rushing up the path to make sure the coast was clear, then running back with a bark to encourage her friends to pick up the pace. From her energy, one would have thought that *her* life depended upon reaching the throne and garnering the wisdom of the Sage.

At the moment, Wiggen was wrestling with his hopes for the Sage's help. Would the Sage have any lifesaving advice to help him dispel the brain fog and soften up the hardened heart from which he suffered? On one hand, he was hopeful to learn the answers that would save his life, and on the other, he feared the possibility that the Sage might not have the cure he had prayed for. He realized now that if the Sage couldn't help him, he would rather *not* know, and instead, go on living in the hope that there was a cure. This is one gift that the quest had provided for him. Facing such a grim and hopeless reality without hope now seemed worse to him than actually dying once had.

"There's something I don't fully understand. Will Matilda's vision, as we witnessed it, definitely come to pass or just *might* it come to pass?" Barnaby asked.

"I would guess that this depends upon the quality of her belief in it happening and whether she is committed to doing what it will take to manifest it into the world," Cromeas commented.

"Do you mean that if the evil forces in the world have a stronger vision than Matilda's, their cynical, destructive visions of hatred, suffering, and death might result instead?" Wiggen wondered.

"That's exactly right," Matilda confirmed. "It's not only dependent upon my own personal vision for the world's future but it also depends upon us inspiring countless others to join in supporting our visions to come to pass."

"Just as I thought," Wiggen sighed. "So, no matter how badly we want it to happen, it will take a whole lot more than just wanting to make it come about."

"We must not only *want* it. We must be *committed* to making it happen. That's part of the problem with our world. Many people want a lot of things. But the wanting has them feel the lacking of the very thing they long for!"

"You lost me," Barnaby objected.

"Well, how many people do you know who *want* to have a heavy chest of gold coins?" she continued.

"Lots of people. Maybe most, I'd guess," Barnaby replied.

"And how many sad people *want* to be happy?"

"All, I'd say."

"And how many overweight people *want* to be thinner?"

"I get it. So, you're saying that wanting it very badly just isn't going to make it happen by itself," Barnaby reasoned.

"Simply *wanting* something isn't enough to make it happen. Wanting something implies not having it," she continued. "So the person who wants something is clear she lacks it and often doesn't expect to have it. So wanting something badly can actually keep it from happening!"

"That's deep!" Wiggen laughed. "But I understand now. You're saying that one must not only want something to happen but actually expect it to happen."

"Yes! Expectation creates self-motivation. And self-motivation will *make* it happen," Matilda went on. "Self-motivation fueled by expectation is at the source of all great accomplishments. If we truly believe that something will happen, we will act in a way that causes it to happen."

"So, are you saying that the opposite is true, too?" Wiggen went on. "If we expect our future to be worse than our present state, we will bring that about too?"

"Yes, we will — through self-sabotage," Matilda affirmed. "It's like the runner who finds himself unexpectedly ahead in the race at the midway point. If he doesn't *expect* to win, he will usually choke and be overtaken by a runner who *does* expect to win and so gives it her all in the home stretch."

"So, if we expect a world filled with hatred and violence, that's what we'll get?" Barnaby chipped in.

"Yes, and if we expect the future to be about the same as the past, our apathy will see that this self-fulfilling prophesy be realized. We gather lots of evidence from our past to predict what our future will bring.

And, this *living in the past* does not support us to define and create a powerful future. We need to *declare* what our future will be like and then go out and make it happen."

"So, this values-based vision needs to start with us and ignite the rest of the world — just like Matilda's vision did!" Cromeas added.

"Yes, our belief in its inevitability, and our bold, consistent, and persistent actions in support of this belief, will inspire others to join us in our dream's realization. That's how all great leaders accomplish magnificent feats," Wiggen agreed. "They motivate and inspire others by declaring what they see as possible and the possible then becomes probable. So, it really is up to us first. I'm committed to it, Matilda!"

"As am I," Cromeas added.

"And I!" Barnaby chimed in.

Just at this moment, Shire ran back to the group, barking and jumping frantically.

"What is it, girl?" Matilda asked.

"We had better proceed cautiously," Wiggen advised.

"Let's get off this path and see if we can get a closer look," Barnaby suggested.

They all edged quietly forward through the trees and brush. The gloom that hid much of the sun's light made it even harder to see what lay ahead, but there was still enough light to see a bit into the distance.

"Look there, high in the cliffs!" Cromeas whispered. "It's the Throne of Noltis!"

The others looked up to see a peculiar sight. There, high upon the cliffside, was the towering rock formation in the shape of a royal throne. It was monumental in size, larger than the largest sports arenas in the land. It was made of a striated red and white rock. At the Throne's base the travelers saw this warning carved deep into the red rock:

Beware: You Have Entered the Domain of the Protectors — Trespassers Will Be Eliminated!

All around lay hundreds of eerie elevated graves with mounds of stones piled high to cover the bodies. Their owners' weapons had been stuck in the ground as markers. Clearly, some unfortunates had chosen to ignore the grim warning.

"I now understand why this place is called 'The Ends of the Earth!'" Barnaby whispered. "It looks like many have already met their ends here."

"It seems we have no choice but to turn back," Cromeas whined in resignation.

"Nonsense!" Wiggen shot back. "Did we all not agree that we were committed to this mission? Are we going to let a little problem stand in our way?"

"This is no *little* problem!" Cromeas objected. "It could mean losing our lives!"

"We all must die sometime. I've come to the realization that there are some things worth risking it all for!" Wiggen replied. "Besides, if we are not successful in manifesting our shared vision for the world, many more of our people will lose their lives through war and violence. To turn back and admit defeat will guarantee that everyone loses."

"Maybe this is a test of our commitment to our vision," Matilda interjected. "Whenever anyone makes a commitment, *problems* always arise. That's just the way life works. Don't you think it is how we respond to these problems that makes the real difference? Some will persevere and align their actions with their commitments, but others will choose the path of convenience and quit when the going gets tough. Well, I don't want to be a quitter."

"I agree!" Wiggen cried. "I see this as just another challenge. We'll overcome this challenge and reach our goal. Too many of our people despair when the going gets too challenging. They trade in their dreams for stagnant resignation. They forget they ever had the possibility of making things happen. They sacrifice their belief in their abilities, and their spirits die a bit more each time they make the choice to settle for less. But we are resolute in pursuing our commitments."

"So, it's onward we go!" Barnaby agreed with his son.

The others clapped their hands in vigorous agreement. Cromeas took out his handkerchief to make a white flag and Barnaby found a long, straight stick to tie it to. With flag held high and Shire by their side, the four returned to the path arm-in-arm. They strode up the side of the mountain and directly toward the menacing warning sign.

"Wouldn't it be wiser to gather some weapons and approach our enemies from a position of force?" Barnaby wondered aloud.

"That was our old way of resolving differences," Cromeas responded. "Remember when we had to be warriors? We would fear the enemy so much that we decided to arm ourselves to the hilt, justifying the violence we inflicted as necessary to defend ourselves from violence. Look around at these grave sites. Every one of them is marked by a weapon. Looks like that strategy didn't work so well, after all!"

"I agree," Wiggen added. "Our strength lies in our vulnerability. Whoever the protectors are, when they see that we are unarmed, hopefully they will allow us the chance to share our vision for peace and harmony. They'll see that our quest is genuine and only contributes to *their* future peace, happiness, and best interests. Besides, aren't we determined to stay true to our ideals in spite of the major risk that lies ahead?"

"We now can fully appreciate the outcome that violence brings, so what do we have to lose?" Barnaby added. "It's really easy to love those who love us back.

A true sign of growth is to love those who hate us. Hatred only generates more hatred in return. If this curse of violence in the world is ever to be lifted, I think it will come from acting out of love and compassion. Besides, I'm beginning to learn that people who get what they want are those who seek out the conditions and circumstances they want. And, if they can't find them, they take responsibility for making them."

"Well said, Barnaby! I think there may still be hope for you yet," Cromeas teased his former adversary.

Empowered by the support he was receiving, Barnaby continued. "I say, don't go around complaining that the world owes you anything. The world was here before you were! And life is not fair. The sooner we understand this, the quicker we'll be able to deal with the real challenges. Whatever doesn't kill you will make you stronger," Barnaby joked with a smile that quickly faded as he remembered that this adventure still might very well yet kill them all.

"My father had a favorite saying when we lived by the sea," Matilda said. "'A ship docked in port is safe and secure, but that's not what ships are made for!'

Besides, I'm learning that safety and security are just an illusion. It is really no safer to live a life that settles for less than it is to go out and make those dreams happen."

Just then, a thundering voice rang out ahead from the red rock perch on the trail above them:

You pay no attention to our most generous warning!
You trespass our lands with such malice and cunning,
Before you can harm us or pass by our door,
You will join those who ignored our warnings before!

"Well, I should have known better. Isn't that always the way? We make a commitment and a problem shows up!" Barnaby whispered.

Wiggen shouted back his immediate reply, "Our white flag flies high. We seek no confrontation. Let us learn of your customs and permit us to tell you of our mission."

The reply from above came back:

Only kin are permitted.
Strangers aren't allowed,
Go back and your skins
May be saved even now!

Wiggen didn't miss a beat in responding, "We will not be denied! I insist you allow us to pass."

As his words were still ringing against the rock, a hand bomb was lobbed from the perch above, exploding just out of range. The travelers were shaken but unharmed.

"It looks to me like insisting isn't going to do the trick!" Matilda said to the others. "Let me try." Then she stepped forward and called out, "We've come a great distance. We are visionary partners on a mission of peace. We seek the Sage's wisdom. Permit us to approach you, for we mean you no harm."

Just then, a goblin sentry perched high above the Throne signaled his urgent need to speak with his commander.

In private, so only the top goblin could hear, he shared, "Sir, from my high perch, I can see that masses are converging upon the Throne from all directions and in great numbers. We will surely be outnumbered soon."

From the time that Barnaby and Cromeas had first spread their invitations on the Plains of Minites to join their pilgrimage to Shelindar, word had passed from person to person and village to village. Everywhere the friends went, they shared their story and invited others to join them in their quest. Before long, word had spread far and wide. The success of getting the word out was now being witnessed as throngs approached in all directions. This happening, though, was yet unknown to the travelers.

Upon learning this news, the commander whispered to the sentry, "The numbers you have seen converging on the Throne tell me that the unity of our adversaries is a fact that we can not continue to oppose. Let us save face and see if there yet may be another way we can deal with the situation. Did she not say that they are the visionary partners? That's it! That's how we can avoid the great bloodshed of our people!"

The commander called out to Matilda, "You are *the* visionary partners the legends tell of? Why didn't you say so before? Please forgive us our poor manners. Come and let us welcome you as friends!"

"That was too easy. Do you think it's a trick?" Barnaby whispered to the others.

"No, he sounds sincere. Perhaps he knows something we do not. Let's trust we can work things out with them," Matilda replied.

The four raised their hands into the air and walked slowly up the path. When they had nearly reached the opening of the perch, a goblin dressed in black from head to toe jumped out from behind the boulder where he was hiding. He stood about 3 feet tall. Sharp triangular teeth dominated his mouth and long earlobes nearly touched his shoulders. A black scarf around his head held back a few long white strands of hair, and he carried at his side a short dagger with a multi-jeweled handle. "There is no need to raise your hands. Please forgive our rude reception. We had no idea that you were the visionaries that our legends have foretold."

Wiggen bowed politely. "Thank you, kind sir. Will you please introduce yourself and tell us more of your legend so that we might know you better."

"Why, of course! I am the guardian of the great stone hall and protector of the Sage. My name is Noltis."

As Noltis spoke, hundreds of other goblins stepped out from their hiding places.

Noltis continued, "The safety and protection of the Sage of Shelindar is our obligation. This duty was passed down to us from generation to generation. It goes back so many years that it is no longer known how the obligation originated. Many have trespassed here. We assume they had come to kidnap the Sage or kill him and put an end to his wisdom. All have failed. It is for this reason that we mistrusted your intentions."

"We assure you our purpose is noble," Matilda answered. "As my pledge, I offer my faithful dog. I would be heartbroken should any harm befall her, so you can be certain that we truly mean what we say. You may return her once you have been satisfied that our mission is peaceful."

"That will not be necessary," Noltis responded with a now trusting smile. "She is a noble animal. This is plain for all to see. The writings foretold of your visit, and we have been awaiting your arrival for many a year. The masses that follow your arrival simply confirmed for us the authenticity of your story. You are most welcome as our honored guests."

Matilda turned to the others and spoke. "Masses, what masses?"

As they looked down the slope, they could now see the many others converging upon the Throne. "My, how word has spread! Did you ever imagine that so many would learn of our quest and decide to join us?" Wiggen asked his friends in surprise.

The goblin leader displayed a complete shift from his previously hostile attitude. He was so sociable that Matilda could hardly tell that he was not accustomed to trusting strangers.

Noltis continued, "Tell us now of your mission," and he pointed first to Wiggen.

"Sir, for much of my life, I was not worthy of your trust. Anger consumed me. Hatred was my constant shadow. I detested others and they detested me. Or, should I say, I *thought* others detested me and *I* detested me, so I therefore vented my anger by hating everyone else. A short time ago, I was diagnosed with the terminal conditions of a hardened heart and a debilitating brain fog. I was given 1 year to live, and so I am just about at the end of my allotted time. I have come for two reasons: first, to seek the Sage's wisdom and to learn if there might be a cure for my afflictions; and also now, most importantly, to learn the secrets as to how we might realize our shared visions. These are, in short, to know if it might be possible to create a different sort of world, a world where violence is forsaken in favor of contribution, where hatred is replaced by love and where the darkness that reins the land gives way to a healing light."

"I thank you, young man, for your transparency. I see that your words are authentic and you now regret your past intolerances. I fear that I and many of my people have shared your foibles and misgivings." Noltis continued, "You shall have your audience with the Sage!"

"Thank you so much, good sir!" Wiggen replied, more hopeful now than he had been for many a day.

"And, what of you others? Do you share this young dwarf's honorable vision?" he asked, looking Matilda, Barnaby, and Cromeas squarely in the eye.

Barnaby took a step forward. "We most certainly do, sir. And we have further visions of our own that complement Wiggen's as well. For you see, I am this young lad's father. Much of his early struggles arose from my oversights and inadequacies as a father. I was obsessed with hatred and shame. This obsession I directed toward our enemies, of which Cromeas was one," nodding his head in Cromeas' direction. "I am proud now to call Cromeas and his people my brothers. It is my vision to include all other peoples in that harmonious brotherhood. In fact, I would delight in adding you and your people to this family."

"Very interesting and well said," Noltis nodded. "And what about you, young lady?"

Matilda smiled and stepped forward. "I have literally stumbled upon your lands, having fallen from the world above with my dog. Through the process of our journey, I have seen the possibility of an entirely different way to think and behave for all people. I see light overcoming darkness, love overtaking hate, cooperation replacing competition, and true peace putting an end to warfare in every land. As we've traveled from afar, we have had many insights that have added detail to this vision, but we seek the Sage's counsel as to how we might manifest it."

Noltis listened attentively, nodding as Matilda spoke. "You shall be the first to seek and obtain the Sage's counsel!" he assured.

"There is one thing that troubles me greatly, if I may continue?" Matilda pleaded. She now realized that the goblins' shift was due not only to their acceptance of the legends that foretold of the group's coming but also to the solidarity they perceived as a result of the many converging upon their position, in support for the travelers.

"Yes, by all means, please ask your question," Noltis encouraged.

"If you have protected the Sage all these years from harm, how is it that you have embraced violence and killing in his name? If he is so wise, how could he allow this to be?" Matilda asked.

"That is a fair question, young miss," Noltis replied. "I said that we have been entrusted with guarding the Sage and keeping him safe. I never said that he has shared his wisdom with us! The Sage is safely locked away in his chambers. No goblin has ever dared intrude on his privacy. It was clearly written that only the Visionary Partners would gain admittance to his wise presence. Tomorrow, we shall journey the remaining way up the path leading to the great hall. Then you shall better understand. For this evening, permit us to entertain you as our honored guests. You shall feast with us and rest up for your historic audience with the Sage in the morning."

That evening, the friends shared their visions in great detail with their goblin hosts. They listened to many a fascinating tale about the wondrous lands of Center Earth, dating back long before the Earth Change, and learned more about the rich culture that characterized this much maligned and misunderstood race.

Noltis continued, "We, goblins, I would imagine, are much like all the other people you have met. We share similar hopes and dreams and are plagued by comparable fears and challenges. We have acquired a bad reputation in many areas of the land. But, please know that we always did the very best we could in dealing with the challenges we encountered. Our people have lived in poverty and oppression for centuries. We have been discriminated against and despised by many without just cause. Our villages have been plundered and our citizens treated like animals by their enemies. In short, we only wanted a better life for our people. Please forgive us for erring on the side of violence and retribution rather than peace and forgiveness. We now see that there may be a better way to live. That way is based on peaceful resolution of our differences with others."

All slept soundly that evening with the contentment that comes from making new friends and clearing up terrible misunderstandings. Everyone expected that the morrow would be a day to remember.

Chapter 13
The Sage of Shelindar

The goblins guarding the Sage's great hall had looked forward to this day ever since they had first populated the red rock region of the Ends of the Earth known as Shelindar. On this day, to honor their visionary guests and to celebrate a new chapter in the history of their world, Noltis and his people planned an elaborate procession and ceremony. Goblins from the entire region sent out word to the far reaches of Center Earth that the Visionary Partners had finally arrived and were to meet the Sage of Shelindar within the great hall's antechamber. For years, the dedicated guardians had scared away all who dared to approach and buried those who had refused to be scared away. Now, the goblin heralds spread word of the gala event that was to take place this very day. All were welcomed and even encouraged to attend and share in the merriment. This abrupt change in hospitality on the part of Noltis and his goblin folk raised many an eyebrow and aroused much curiosity.

Matilda, Cromeas, Barnaby, and Wiggen arose to the sound of hundreds of goblin trumpeters, spread out across the land in all directions for as far as one could see, blasting their magnificent call of welcome in unison. Shire had gone on to the stone hall before the others, accompanying Noltis as he made his celebratory preparations.

"I can't believe we are finally going to meet the Sage today!" Wiggen shouted, unable to contain his excitement. "I just know he'll tell me what I can do to cure my terrible condition."

"And I can't wait to learn what it will take to annihilate the gloom!" Matilda added. "Our worlds have been through so very much, but we're finally going to learn how to lift the gloom and how to manifest our vision of light, love, and harmony today!"

"I'm going to ask the Sage how I can be a great communicator of fun in the world," Cromeas proclaimed.

"And I'll ask him how I can inspire others to be as good a friend as I plan on being to everyone," Barnaby added.

With all the commotion involved in preparing for the great event, the morning hours passed rapidly. It was nearly noon when Noltis' messenger sent for Matilda and the others. They made their way up the carved stone stairs, across the Throne of Shelindar to the great stone hall's entrance, carved from the mountainside's red rock ages ago. Some say it had been carved by expert craftsmen who first discovered the region. Others swear it was the handiwork of alien beings from beyond the stars. No matter how it came to be, all who saw it agreed that it was a truly magnificent work of art and beauty.

Matilda's jaw dropped in awe as she approached the entrance. Never had she seen a place so grand. Shire trotted up to meet her and then kept pace by her side. Wiggen, Barnaby, and Cromeas trailed a step behind. As the group stepped inside the stone hall's doorway, they saw that the chamber's inner ceiling stood a lofty 18 stories tall. Dim light was cast from the many great black iron lanterns hanging on both sides of the hall every 30 paces. The lanterns hung from highly polished, rounded, striated red and white stone archways that connected the walls. A series of six symmetrical columns of intricately carved wooden benches were spread out to fill the floor of the great hall.

The friends led the procession down the center path of the stone hall. Glancing back, they were moved to see the rows of benches being filled with scores of men and women, goblins, dwarves, elves, and other races, all journeying from every village and countryside across the many lands of Center Earth.

"I had no idea it would be like this," Barnaby whispered to Cromeas as they made their way to the front of the immense hall.

As the group finally reached the front, a series of three trumpet blasts acknowledged their arrival. Before them, within a smooth opening cut into the surrounding rock, stood a large oak door that was secured by a heavy iron lock. At the base of the door was an iron plaque. The friends bent down to read the preliminary inscription:

For the Visionary Partners Only!
No matter what gender or race,
All others can knock 'til they're blue in the face!

The actual plaque message below this read:

To end all GLOOM, suffering, and fear,
The answer to this riddle lies awfully near.
To cease all hatred, warfare, and rage,
One must seek the wisdom held by the Sage,
The answers you search for lie close at hand,
Always sheltered from evil
And awaiting love to command.
If this vision of peace,
in your heart, you hold dear,
Knock thrice and enter,
And the Sage shall appear!

Matilda looked over at the others. "Could it be so simple?" she asked.

"We are partners with a vision! Knock three times and we shall see," Barnaby urged.

Matilda raised her right hand and struck upon the oak door three times.

The old iron lock fell to the floor and the door swung open.

The four looked at each other with widened eyes. Without uttering a word, Matilda crossed the threshold, followed by Shire, Wiggen, Barnaby, and Cromeas. Cromeas came last, and as he entered the darkened chamber, the door slammed shut behind them.

"Well, I can't say I like that very much!" Cromeas muttered apprehensively.

They inched forward in darkness, bumping into each other as they groped for the walls.

"Is the Sage here?" Wiggen yelled.

A bright beam of warm, golden light suddenly illuminated the room.

"That's sunlight!" Barnaby gasped after blinking in the glare. As their eyes grew used to the long-lost brilliance of sunlight, the friends suddenly realized that they were not standing in a room at all!

Matilda looked around to recognize that she stood next to Shire, with her toes covered by the pink sands of her favorite beach back in the world above. Wiggen stood knee-deep in the tranquil waters of his favorite fishing hole in the Iopu Valley. Barnaby found himself lying in the tall grass beneath the old willow tree in the world above where he would often escape from life's struggles as a child. Now he stared up at the same blue sky that he vividly remembered from his childhood days long ago. Cromeas found himself sitting high in the tree-house his father had built for him as a child. Each looked around but could see no sign of any of the others.

Wiggen looked around and shouted, "Where am I?" at the top of his lungs.

He heard a gentle voice respond, "You are home."

"Where is the Sage of Shelindar?" he exclaimed. "I must find him."

Immediately Wiggen was surrounded by mirrors on all sides of him.

"What is this trickery?" he yelled.

The same gentle voice replied, "It is not trickery. Why is your first thought still so often that you are being tricked? You asked for the Sage and here you have your answer."

"Why, I see only images of myself," Wiggen protested. "And who is the voice I am hearing?"

"You requested the Sage," came back the gentle reply.

"You mean to say that *I* am the Sage we all have sought on our long journey?" he asked. "That's just not possible. The Sage is ancient and wise."

"You are the Sage that *you* seek," came the reply. "The others have met *their* own Sages."

"But what about my fatal conditions? Is there no cure for my brain fog and my hardened heart?" he asked. "I really don't want to die. I have so much to give others now."

"Those infirmities, like all others, were only an outer manifestation of your true inner self. But you've shared love and compassion with yourself and others. Feel the difference! Your heart is no longer hardened. Your brain seems quite free of fog! The lessons you have learned on your journey have done much to reverse these conditions. Continue to keep your mind focused on those lessons and open to all possibilities. Freely share the gift of love from your heart and speak to the love residing in the hearts of others. By doing so, your heart shall be bathed in love and shall remain soft, healthy, and fully open."

"Then, I'm not dying? I'm not dying!" he shouted joyfully.

The answer he heard immediately was, "You're right, Wiggen. You have just recently begun living!"

"And what of my vision? What of Matilda's and Cromeas' and Barnaby's?"

"Are you not already living and manifesting your visions?" the voice responded.

"Why, I now can see that we certainly *are* doing that!" Wiggen said.

The voice continued, "You have doubted yourself. You have ignored your intuition and reacted to external triggers that drowned out your small, inner voice. Know that you can find the answers within and that the questions you pose are of more value than the answers you seek. True growth starts with thoughtful questions. Know, too, that the journey holds the keys. There is no ultimate arrival, for once we reach one answer, we find ourselves on just one more step along another journey."

Listening to the quiet answers, Wiggen gradually found he could no longer distinguish it from his own voice. He decided to listen to his intuition and realized that he was and had always been his own Sage.

While Wiggen was having his breakthrough in self-awareness, Matilda was back on her favorite beach, soon to become reacquainted with her own Sage.

Matilda closed her eyes and spoke into the waves splashing at her feet, "If the Sage is out there, allow yourself to be known."

Matilda opened her eyes and looked down into the water to see a masked figure approaching toward the surface. She reached down, removed the mask and fell back in surprise to see it was *she* behind the mask. But the person she saw appeared more radiant and glorified that she knew herself to be. Matilda soon realized that she was looking at her enlightened self. She glowed with an inner light that was brighter than the brightest star on the clearest night.

"Am I to understand that *you* are my Sage?" she asked.

"You are correct," came her reply.

"Are you all knowing?" she questioned.

"Knowledge is available on many levels. The deeper you look, the more answers you will find," she replied.

"Then, please tell me, how can I vanquish the gloom? Will I achieve my vision of bringing peace and harmony to all lands?"

She immediately heard the reply, "Your questions are the same. You know that you have the power to lift the gloom and manifest this vision. Your answer depends upon your commitment to make it be so."

Matilda needed to ask no more questions at that time. She knew instinctively that she would need to communicate more with her inner Sage for guidance in all areas of her life. She knew what she must do — more of what she *had* already been doing over the course of her journey. She trusted that the answers to questions she would have along the way would be there when she looked within. No need to fret about that now. It was time to enjoy the process and spread the light and love to every dark corner of the world.

Barnaby was surprised to find out that the Sage was not an ancient wise man waiting to instruct him.

"Who are you? What can you tell me?" he asked.

"I am your inner voice," came his reply. "You gave up on trusting yourself so long ago. It is never too late to hear your inner voice and trust your inner wisdom."

To Barnaby, this whole notion was both scary and exciting at once!

"But I do not know where to begin. How will I know what I should do?" he asked

"You have the answers to all your questions within you," he heard in reply.

"But I don't even know what questions to ask!" Barnaby protested.

"Then you shall need to look more closely at those areas where you find struggle, unhappiness, and suffering in your life and in the lives of those around you. There are many questions there awaiting your inquiry. Determine what your questions are and then listen to your intuition for your answers. It is this inner knowing that you must further develop and learn to trust."

Barnaby was beginning to understand. "I resolve to develop and strengthen my intuition day by day. I imagine this will be just like building up a weak muscle. And I have done that before, after being injured in battle. I know that each day will bring me a higher level of personal development and awareness. I also know that I have a great coach in my beloved son, Wiggen, should I ever again become confused and lose sight of my personal power." These thoughts brought Barnaby an inner peace greater than he had ever known.

Cromeas struggled initially when encountering his Sage.

"Upon first hearing the voice, he protested, "You say that I am my own Sage? Why, that can't possibly be true. I lack the wisdom that all sages must have."

"It is true. Trust in your wisdom," came his reply.

"I refuse to believe that the true source of wisdom could possibly be within me," he stubbornly persisted.

"Believe it, for it is indeed true," came his reply yet again.

"What proof do you have?" he challenged.

"For those who believe, no proof is necessary. For those who doubt, no proof is possible," came his answer.

"Are you saying that I must believe you?" Cromeas continued.

"I am saying that you must believe in yourself!" came his response.

"But how?" he challenged.

"Your answers are within, awaiting your discovery. Trust that they are there and listen to that small, still, knowing voice whenever you seek guidance," his Sage replied.

And so, after such a lengthy internal debate, his voice of reason finally prevailed, always patiently reminding him that *he* was the man he sought. After several affirmations reminding him of his inner Sage, he finally got it — at least for the present time!

"Very well. I think I now understand. My intuition tells me that it's all right for me to still be a bit confused. My answers will eventually come if I continue searching for them. I commit to the lifelong pursuit of personal development in partnership with my good friend, Barnaby. We were once two of the most stubborn and ignorant warriors around. I suppose if we can reinvent ourselves to live our values and share our gifts, so could anyone," he reasoned.

When each of the four had been properly reintroduced to their inner strength and source of wisdom, the exotic illusions evaporated into the ether, and they found themselves back within a private room within the great stone hall of Shelindar.

Chapter 14
The Light of a New Era Dawns

Matilda, Wiggen, Cromeas, and Barnaby looked at each other with the shared, unspoken knowledge that comes when people reach life-changing insights together. Each emitted a glow that filled the entire room in which they found themselves standing. With all four of them in the same room, the radiance was almost blinding! As the friends emerged from their private room and entered the great stone hall, the brilliant illumination continued to emanate from them, soon filling the entire hall with bright light.

"What a glorious day! My only regret is that my mother couldn't be here to experience it with us," Matilda told the others. As she spoke these words, she reached for the amulet she wore around her neck. Opening it, she struck the tinder box and a bright light filled the great hall.

In that instant, the blind beggar who had first greeted Wiggen on his path appeared. He bowed in reverence before the group. Without saying a word, within moments, he was magically transformed into the wise old woman the friends had met along their journey and in the cave. The old woman likewise bowed her head in a sign of respect. A few moments later, she vanished and Tonesia was standing there in her place.

Matilda stood there for several moments with her mouth opened, mesmerized and unable to speak. Finally, she spoke, "Mother! That was you all along?"

"Did I not tell you that I would be with you always, my dear?" she asked with a fond smile. "Messages do not always come to us in the packages we expect them to!"

"Mother! Of course, you are with me always. How could I have doubted this? But I never expected you could assume various shapes and assist me in my quest by taking the guise of others! Can you believe the events that are happening this day? Are they not magnificent?" Matilda asked with a gleam in her eye.

"They are indeed, my darling. And you have yet to witness the most grand of them all," Tonesia replied with outstretched arms facing the throng that had gathered to witness the appearance of the Sage. The hall was filled with people from every land of Center Earth as well as many originally from lands in the world above. While Matilda, Wiggen, Barnaby, and Cromeas were experiencing breakthrough conversations with their inner sages, each of the people in the great hall also had experienced a similar audience with *their* own personal sages.

Pointing to the masses that filled the great hall, Tonesia declared, "Each of these people now know that they too can turn to their own inner sages to reach the wisdom that they will need to lead rich lives of passion and purpose."

Tonesia then raised her voice. "Let us acknowledge these four brave souls whose courage and visions have brought a new chapter filled with endless possibilities to our world!" At these words, the throng rose to their feet and applauded wildly. Tonesia then led Matilda and the others in a procession through the crowd. The crowd chanted and cheered as the visionary partners made their way slowly back outside to the Throne.

Tonesia waved in all directions and spoke again. "Behold the seeds of your vision, Matilda, Wiggen, Cromeas, and Barnaby!"

Matilda glowed as if surrounded by a thousand torches. Directly above her head, the gloom in the sky was pierced with a bolt of lightening. At first, it opened up a small hole through which bright sunlight streamed forth, exposing the clear, blue sky behind it. Soon, the light spread in the sky above each person's head. As the gloom lifted, joy and love filled the hearts of those witnessing the spectacle. In miraculous fashion, the light in the sky spread from person to person and soon, from ridge to ridge, within minutes igniting the entire countryside in the same way a fire might spread rapidly through a dry forest. People gathered throughout the valley below in all directions. Their spirits soared as the late afternoon sky was illuminated across the land with the sun's healing rays.

As the miracle continued to unfold and afternoon passed into night, Matilda lit a large lantern and hung it upon a post by the great hall's door. From this lantern, a great number of other lanterns were lit to signify the light that was spreading throughout the land as well as within the hearts of the people. Before long, word had spread everywhere of the friends' noble vision and mission.

After unhitching her lantern from the post, Matilda held it high above her head and proclaimed, "Let everyone in every village and in every cave light a lantern with these flames to mark a new dawn for the people of the world!"

In the same way that the gloom had disappeared earlier in the day, spreading from person to person and area to area, so too was Matilda's lantern's light spread. Soon, the evening countryside was all aglow with lanterns ignited from flames that had all originated from Matilda's lantern. As each lantern was ignited, so too was sparked an internal flame in the heart of its owner, a heart now open to the healing light and love that was spreading throughout the world.

A small boy ran up to Matilda and said, "Oh, great Light-Bearer, my torch has blown out!" Matilda touched him with her finger extended and soon his torch was reignited and the area around him was aglow in light.

As twilight approached the Throne and the crowd standing in the valley below, Matilda could still see the colors of the Ishites mingling with the colors of the Plabians. She knew that the peace that Barnaby and

Cromeas had begun that day on the Plains of Minites had spread from person to person in a massive rippling effect. A representative from each side lit their lanterns with the flame that came from Matilda's lantern. Before long, that flame was spread from person to person, igniting all lanterns to spread a warm and brilliant glow.

Wiggen looked out and recognized the colors of Nimi and his elves. Nimi's people were inspired by Matilda's vision for peace and had spread this vision among all the different races. They told every elf, dwarf, human, and goblin they could find. The start of a new consciousness among many previously warring people resulted from this group's inspiration.

To the west, Barnaby pointed out Karbon's goblin factions. They were rejoicing arm-in-arm with Noltis' followers, their old adversaries. Those who had once been considered bitter enemies of all other races now embraced the vision of brotherhood and friendship. And so it was everywhere one looked — goblins and elves, men and dwarves, whether previously strangers or even prior enemies for centuries, it mattered not. All were inspired by the possibilities of Matilda's and Wiggen's visions.

As night fell upon the Enchantment Mountains and the valley below, millions of brightly lit torches and lanterns illuminated the sky in concentric circles for as far as the eye could see. "This is the scene I saw at the Vision Pool!" Matilda exclaimed. "Our vision is indeed coming to pass, though I had no idea how it could manifest!"

"Your courage to inspire those you meet and their courage to inspire all they meet formed the foundation for the movement that you see has taken hold here this day," Tonesia explained. "Global transformation can only occur with one personal transformation at a time. With the power of geometric progression, you four soon inspired 16, who inspired 64 others, who went on to inspire 256, and so forth. With the awesome power made possible by a lot of people each doing a little bit, your message soon reached millions. And this is just the beginning! I expect that this progression will continue to touch every life in this world, if not those still living in the world above, as well. Soon, you will witness that as news spreads, the atmosphere across our land and in the world above is no longer fouled with the gloom caused by evil forces and dark thoughts. It will have been cleansed from the inner glow of enlightenment that so many will possess."

Noltis stepped to the center of the Throne that bore his name. In his hands was an iron lantern that had been posted by the gate. Offering his lantern to Matilda, he said, "Oh, Light-Bearer, please share your light." Request after similar request followed. And so, it was that all were inspired and touched by the light that spread from person to person that day.

Noltis continued, "On behalf of an inspired and grateful people from every land reaching from the Restless Wilds in the north to the Slather in the southwest to here where we stand at the Ends of the Earth, I request that you, Lady Matilda, and you, Sir Wiggen, accept the gratitude of your people. What this brave, new world needs is courageous leadership marked by integrity. I hereby propose the coronation of our own, King Wiggen I!"

At these words, the crowd erupted with a thunderous roar that was heard in every corner of the land. "Long live the King! Long live the King!" they shouted.

Matilda turned and looked at Wiggen. "They couldn't have made a better choice!" she said.

Wiggen turned to face the crowd and said, "I can't believe this is actually happening! With humility and a loving heart, on behalf of all people in every land of Center Earth, I, your humble servant, do graciously accept this honor and pledge to you my undying commitment to serve you so that you might better serve others!"

Wiggen looked with sincere appreciation at Matilda and then at the crowd. He shouted, "My first act as your king will be to appoint my dear friend, Matilda as the peoples' ambassador!"

"Long live Matilda the Light-Bearer!" shouted the crowd.

Matilda smiled and replied, "My first proclamation as your goodwill ambassador is this: In every village and on every farm, cave, or mountaintop, wherever people gather, let there be set a lantern that shall take its flame from one of the torches and lanterns lit here this great day. And let it be known to one and to all that for as long as that lantern's flame shall glow brightly, let there be peace and harmony in each of our hearts, in each of our homes and in each of our lands!"

The crowd's roar of jubilation was nothing short of deafening. Celebrations throughout the land continued on that evening and for many weeks to come. In each town or countryside gathering, the people earnestly carried out Matilda's request. Lanterns were hung as symbols of the light and love by which the people would forever illuminate their lives. Songs were written and parades were held to commemorate each lantern's installation. The light glowing from each lantern filled each person's heart with joy and love. Each adopted Matilda's and Wiggin's visions for a world marked by peace and harmony. Many created inspired visions of their own. So great was the transformation that resulted that it yielded one thousand years in which peace reigned over the land.

True to their words, Barnaby and Cromeas fully championed Matilda's and Wiggen's visions. Cromeas gave up the whining he had been known for and spent his remaining days communicating his own new zest for life while showing others how to have fun too. Barnaby lived his life purpose of being a friend to others, especially those in need of one. His friendship with his former adversary, Cromeas, inspired many to rethink their self-righteous positions if they thought about dominating others.

Wiggen's reign went down in the annals as the Golden Years of Center Earth. Never before had this realm known such prosperity, peace, and cooperation among different factions. He ruled with the heartfelt compassion and clarity of purpose that characterizes truly great leaders. Those who knew him best were always amazed at how he could have once suffered from the debilitating ailments of a hardened heart and a foggy brain.

As ambassador, Matilda commissioned many a project in search of a way back to the world above. However, all efforts to do so failed. However, with the help of her mother, Tonesia, she was able to send word of the glorious happenings throughout Center Earth back to her father, Costas. Through her mother's magical assistance, Matilda and her father were able to communicate freely through the hot springs that flowed from Center Earth to the world above. Many passing these springs reported hearing their voices in the bubbling waters.

Matilda worked tirelessly to spread her message of light and love across the land. Everywhere she went, she defeated resignation and gloom and inspired hope, communication, and brotherhood. Though her many good works were heralded as remarkable throughout the land, she was still best remembered for the time when the sky first became illuminated and the gloom disappeared. As she traveled the land, small children pointed to her in awe and said, "Look, there goes Matilda the Light-Bearer!" Before long, the legend grew as all came to share the tale of how the light was spread from person to person and village to village.

Though Matilda missed her father and even her old homeland, she came to realize that she had landed in Center Earth for a very good reason. "Nothing happens by accident," she would often remind herself. It was there, in Center Earth, that she could do the most good. This she did daily with the joy of one living in harmony with her life purpose.

Costas, too, was inspired to step into leadership in the world above. He rallied the remaining villagers in his community with all the other survivors of the Earth

Change he could find. They resolved to rebuild their world upon the same peaceful model his daughter had inspired. They spread the good news of harmonious coexistence from place to place and inspired survivors everywhere to live in peace and contribution to others.

Some time after his coronation as king over the united territories of Center Earth, Wiggen left the hustle and bustle of court to visit his old friend, Cromeas. There he finally set eyes upon Kuchina. The two quickly found that they shared a growing love and a vision for a better world, so Wiggen and Kuchina were married with great celebration. The royal couple proved to be compassionate rulers, and Queen Kuchina spearheaded many philanthropic projects that spread light and harmony throughout the kingdom.

For nearly 1,000 peaceful years in Center Earth, war was a forgotten practice only read of in the history scrolls. The time came, while all Center Earth celebrated a new millenia, that the first king and queen left their thrones to their children and quietly retired. Wiggen and Kuchina slipped from public view to live a simple life in a region called the Land of Endless Possibilities.

In their cottage, Kuchina encouraged Wiggen to pen his extensive memoirs, writings which also proved him to be a gifted seer. He predicted that the long peace of his reign would continue, but eventually would be broken by periods of discord for ages to come. After all, people's shortcomings are never permanently subdued, and once someone forgets to manage his dark side, trouble is bound to follow. So, Wiggen wrote, mankind would gradually forget the hard lessons learned and eventually fall back into the old ways of fear, competition, and unrelenting domination.

In the midst of his dire foretellings, Wiggen promised that benevolent leaders would still arise to alternate with the cruel, evil tyrants. He also predicted, a little mysteriously, that once his beloved world succumbed to its violent ignorance of old, he just might be compelled to find a way to return and set things straight again.

Although many fondly chuckled over these writings as the colorful delusions of an amusing old man, Center Earth's learned scribes meticulously copied Wiggen's predictions and preserved sets of these scrolls in secret locations across the kingdom.

And so Wiggen and Kuchina lived out their remaining years together in joyous love and satisfaction. More years passed, more kings and queens came and went, and ignorance indeed gradually overshadowed enlightenment. Before anyone actually realized the loss, the hard lessons recounted in these adventures became forgotten. But somehow, the triumphant legend of the light-bearers lingered, undimmed. And its transformational power continues, even as *this* tale ends.

Dr. Joe Rubino is widely acknowledged as one of North America's foremost success and productivity coaches. He is the CEO of Visionary International Partnerships. People throughout the world have benefited from his books, tapes, coaching, and leadership development training. Together with Dr. Tom Ventullo, he is the co-founder of The Center for Personal Reinvention, an organization that provides coaching and productivity and leadership development courses that champion people to maximize their personal power and effectiveness. Dr. Rubino's books are available in 14 languages and in 43 countries.

Also by Dr. Joe Rubino:
The Power to Succeed: 30 Principles for Maximizing Your Personal Effectiveness
The Power to Succeed: More Principles for Powerful Living, Book II
The Magic Lantern: A Fable About Leadership, Personal Excellence and Empowerment
Restore Your Magnificence: A Life-Changing Guide to Reclaiming Your Self-Esteem
Secrets of Building A Million Dollar Network Marketing Organization from A Guy Who's Been There, Done That and Shows You How to Do It Too.
10 Weeks to Network Marketing Success: The Secrets to Launching Your Very Own Million-Dollar Organization in A 10-Week Business-Building and Personal-Development Self-Study Course (4 CDs and workbook)

To request information about any of The Center for Personal Reinvention's programs or to order any of Dr. Rubino's books, visit http://www.CenterForPersonalReinvention.com

Recommended Personal Development Programs

The Center for Personal Reinvention

Dr. Joe Rubino and Dr. Tom Ventullo

Where are you blocked in your life and in your business?

Where is there an unacceptable level of resignation or conflict?

Where are there interpersonal listening and communications skills lacking?

Where are you lacking partnership, commitment, and vision?

The world we live and work in is marked by unprecedented change and fraught with new and complex challenges. For many of us, life begins to look like an uphill struggle to survive instead of a fun and exciting opportunity to grow, risk, and live our dreams in partnership with others. The stresses, conflicts, and frustrations we experience daily need not be so.

There exists another possibility.

...To live and work with passion — empowered by the challenges of life.

...To champion others to achieve excellence in a nurturing environment that fosters partnerships.

...To acquire the success principles that support affinity, creativity, and harmony.

...To listen and communicate in such a way that others can see new possibilities for accomplishment, partnership, and excellence.

Reinventing ourselves and our relationships by challenging and changing our perception of the world is the result of a never-ending commitment to our own personal magnificence and to that of others. It is made possible through practicing approximately 50 key principles that completely shift your view of life and others. When people really *get* these principles, life, relationships, and new possibilities for breakthroughs show up from a totally fresh perspective. Through the use of cutting-edge technology as a vibrant basis for learning, growing, and acting, The Center for Personal Reinvention successfully supports people to view life with a new and fresh awareness as they self-discover these life-changing principles.

With this program, YOU will:

*Uncover the secrets to reaching your personal power while maximizing your productivity.

*Gain clarity on exactly what it will take to reach your goals with velocity.

* Create a structure for boosting your effectiveness while developing new and empowering partnerships.

* Learn how taking total responsibility for every aspect of your life and business can result in breakthrough performance.

* Discover the key elements of a detailed action plan and how to reach your goals in record time.

*Acquire the keys to listening and communicating effectively and intentionally.

*Recognize and shift out of self-defeating thoughts and actions.

*Gain the insight to better understand others with new compassion and clarity.

*Learn how to develop the charisma necessary to attract others to you.

*Experience the confidence and inner peace that comes from stepping into leadership.

The Center for Personal Reinvention... Transferring the Power to Succeed!

Customized Courses and Programs

Personally Designed For Achieving Maximum Results

Areas of Focus Include:

Designing Your Future
Making Life and Businesses Work
Generating Infinite Possibilities
Creating Conversations for Mutuality and Exploring Common Ground
Commitment Management
Personal Coaching and Development
Maximizing Personal Effectiveness
Breakthrough Productivity
Leadership Development
Relationship and Team Building
Conflict Resolution
Listening for Solutions
Systems for Personal Empowerment

Personal and Productivity Transformation
Designing Structures for Accomplishment
Creating Empowered Listening Styles
Possibility Thinking
Moving Life in a Forward Direction
Structures for Team Accountability
Innovative Thinking
Completing with the Past
Creating a Life of No Regrets

The Center for Personal Reinvention champions companies and individuals to achieve their potential through customized programs addressing specific needs consistent with their vision for the future.

Contact us today to explore
how we might impact your world!

The Center for Personal Reinvention
PO Box 217,
Boxford, MA 01921
drjrubino@email.com
Tel: (888) 821-3135
Fax: (630) 982-2134

Personal and Group Coaching Programs

The Value of Coaching to Support Your Business and Your Life

In our daily lives as well as in our businesses, we typically deal with life's challenges the best we know how. If we knew what it would take to be more effective in our relationships, more productive in our activities, or more successful in reaching our goals, we would surely change accordingly. The only openings we ordinarily have to impact our lives comes from the areas of "what we know" and "what we don't know." In our efforts to achieve more, we usually resort to increasing what we do know by learning to do things a little better, a little differently or we simply repeat a behavior that produced a certain result for us in the past. This behavior can produce small, incremental increases in our ability to impact our business and our world. Likewise, by educating ourselves in the arena of "what we don't know," this knowledge then becomes part of what we now do know: If you are computer illiterate and you learn how to adeptly operate a computer, you will have successfully converted something that you do not know into what you now know. More than 95 percent of our efforts are spent in these two arenas – what we know and what we don't know.

However, our most extraordinary growth comes from outside the arena of what we know or don't know. What lies beyond is the vast array of ideas that we are blind to, not knowing that they even exist. It's in this arena of "what we don't know we don't know" that we can make our greatest breakthroughs.

So how do you gain access to this fertile territory if you don't even know that it exists? The answer lies in recruiting the help of a coach who can support you to explore outside of your customary perspective and behaviors. Your coaches should be individuals who possess the key principles that make them powerful in the particular arena they offer coaching. A coach may be powerful in some arenas but not necessarily in others. The same person who is qualified to coach you in business matters may be totally unqualified to coach you in the area of relationships or spiritual matters. True coaches do not give advice or lend their opinions. They are value based, not ego based. They do not manipulate or exploit to carry out their own agenda. They are totally nonjudgmental. They are not the same as counselors or therapists. They do not try to protect, control, or rescue those they are coaching. They instead listen for where you may be experiencing challenges or may be missing some element that's a key for desired change. Coaches support us in seeing something that we may not be aware of by listening both to what we say and to what we leave out. They empathize with the person being coached, but they are not emotionally attached to any particular outcome. They champion people to have their lives work optimally. They do this by asking questions, exploring possibilities, making requests, and, at times, confronting issues that may need to be examined. Skilled coaching is a fine art and a highly valuable service.

For a coaching relationship to be possible, there *must* exist an open willingness on the part of the person being coached to endure and actively participate in the process. Of course, total confidentiality must exist to allow for the freedom to explore any and all areas necessary. The absence of judging and advice creates the openness needed to fully examine any possibility.

Coaching typically addresses any of six major areas of life: business/career, health, wealth, relationships, spirituality/personal development, or recreation/passions. A good coach will clarify if the coaching client is open to explore any or all of these areas or if the coaching relationship is agreed to be specifically limited to certain areas. True coaches interact with honor and respect while staying ready to call someone on their "stuff," all out of a solid commitment to champion the person's excellence and best interests.

Successful coaches:

Listen for what may be missing to accomplish a result or honor a person's values.

Lead by example and champion others to step into leadership.

Are committed to their client's excellence without becoming attached to his or her responses.

Are grounded in value-based personal development principles.

Hold those they coach as totally capable and competent while looking for what might be missing for them to fully experience their magnificence.

Nurture the client to be their best and live with passion while accomplishing their goals.

Never make the client feel small or dependent.

Champion the coaching client to be the best they can be while staying "invisible" as a coach. The coach's ego must not be a factor in the relationship.

Tell the truth and do not skirt uncomfortable topics or situations in order to avoid discomfort or look good.

Create a safe atmosphere that allows the client to be vulnerable and open to possibilities.

Support their coaching clients in an accountability structure, ensuring that they follow through on what they say they will do.

Support the free flow of ideas and conversations for possibilities through idea streaming.

It is helpful for any coaching relationship to begin by developing clarity with respect to the client's overall vision. This vision should include every aspect of the person's life and business. From this wide-ranging perspective, it is then possible to develop a plan to accomplish any goals. These goals blend into the big picture by fulfilling or working toward one aspect of the vision's realization.

A productive coaching relationship can focus on either a life or business project. In the realm of business or network marketing, a coaching relationship is often best undertaken within the context of a project or action plan that is grounded in a specific timeframe. By focusing on producing specific and measurable results, a coach can support a client to best work through any business or personal challenges en route to accomplishing one's goals. A coach can also assist in gaining clarity on all conditions of satisfaction that may be important to a project's fulfillment. Such conditions might include those non-measurable items that would need to take place for a project to be considered a success. These might include developing stronger relationships with family members, spending quality time with children, devoting a minimum amount of daily time to meeting one's own needs, taking a well deserved vacation, etc.

Many people mistakenly assume that they can be successful in business without being successful in other areas of their lives. While important, our businesses are only one component of our lives. If there is an imbalance in any of the six prominent areas of our lives, any business accomplishment will be somehow incomplete. For this reason, a good coach will support a client to adopt a whole-thinking perspective with mastery of all areas of life as the ultimate goal. For this reason, personal development is an essential component of any business coaching relationship. As one undertakes the personal improvement process, increased business productivity will surely result.

Just as an Olympic athlete in pursuit of a gold medal would not think of aiming for such an accomplishment without the support of a coach, most people would likewise benefit from a coaching relationship. Coaching can add fun and excitement to every aspect of your life as you take on the challenge of reinventing yourself and your business, always in search of excellence. And of course, one of the major benefits of an ongoing coaching relationship is that you will develop the coaching skills yourself that will be necessary for you to impact the lives of others, who will likewise look to you for coaching. If you are in business and do not yet have a coach who is committed to championing your success, I strongly encourage you to look into how such a relationship might support your goals and move your business and life forward with velocity.

Hire a Coach

The Center for Personal Reinvention offers individual and group coaching programs that support people to realize their business and life goals while designing lives of choice, without regrets. For more information on hiring a coach, please contact Dr. Joe Rubino at DrJRubino@email.com or by calling (888) 821-3135.

Other Books by Dr. Joe Rubino

The Power to Succeed: 30 Principles for Maximizing Your Personal Effectiveness

What exactly distinguishes those who are effective in their relationships, productive in business and happy, powerful, and successful in their approach to life from those who struggle, suffer, and fail? That is the key question that *The Power to Succeed: 30 Principles for Maximizing Your Personal Effectiveness* explores in life-changing detail. The information, examples, experiences, and detailed exercises offered will produce life-altering insights for readers who examine who they *are being* on a moment-to-moment basis that either contributes to increasing their personal effectiveness, happiness, and power — or not. As you commit to an inquiry around what it takes to access your personal power, you will gain the tools to overcome any challenges or limiting thoughts and behavior and discover exactly what it means to be the best you can be.

With this book YOU will:
Uncover the secrets to accessing your personal power.
Create a structure for maximizing your effectiveness with others.
Learn to take total responsibility for everything in your life.
Discover the key elements to accomplishment and how to reach your goals in record time.
Identify your life rules and discover how honoring your core values can help you maximize productivity.
Complete your past and design your future on purpose.

Discover the keys to communicating effectively and intentionally.
Stop complaining and start doing.
Seize your personal power and conquer resignation in your life.
Learn how to generate conversations that uncover new possibilities.
See how embracing problems can lead to positive breakthroughs in life.
Leave others whole while realizing the power of telling the truth.
Learn how to develop the charisma necessary to attract others to you.

The Magic Lantern: A Fable about Leadership, Personal Excellence and Empowerment

Set in the magical world of Center Earth, inhabited by dwarves, elves, goblins, and wizards, *The Magic Lantern* is a tale of personal development that teaches the keys to success and happiness. This fable examines what it means to take on true leadership while learning to become maximally effective with everyone we meet.

Renowned personal development trainer, coach, and veteran author, Dr. Joe Rubino tells the story of a group of dwarves and their young leader who go off in search of the secrets to a life that works, a life filled with harmony and endless possibilities and void of the regrets and upsets that characterize most people's existence. With a mission to restore peace and harmony to their village in turmoil, the characters overcome the many challenges they encounter along their eventful journey. Through self-discovery, they develop the principles necessary to be the best that they can be as they step into leadership and lives of contribution to others.

The Magic Lantern teaches us:
The power of forgiveness
The meaning of responsibility and commitment
What leadership is really all about
The magic of belief and positive expectation
The value of listening as an art
The secret to mastering one's emotions and actions
And much more.

It combines spellbinding storytelling with the personal development tools of the great masters.

The Power to Succeed: More Principles for Powerful Living, Book II

This revealing book continues where *The Power to Succeed: 30 Principles for Maximizing Your Personal Effectiveness* left off with more powerful insights into what it takes to be most happy, successful and effective with others.

With this book YOU will:
Discover the keys to unlock the door to success and happiness
Learn how your listening determines what you attract to you.
And how to shift your listening to access your personal power.

See how creating a clear intention can cause miracles to show up around you.

Learn the secrets to making powerful requests to get what you want from others.

Discover how to fully connect with and champion others to realize their greatness.

Learn to create interpretations that support your excellence and avoid those that keep you small.

Develop the power to speak and act from your commitments.

See how communication with others can eliminate unwanted conditions from your life.

Discover the secret to being happy and eliminating daily upsets.

Learn how to put an end to gossip and stop giving away your power.

Develop the ability to lead your life with direction and purpose and discover what it's costing you not to do so.

And More!!

The Power to Succeed: 30 Principles for Maximizing Your Personal Effectiveness and its sequel, *The Power to Succeed: More Principles for Powerful Living, Book II*, are a powerful course in becoming the person you wish to be. Read these books, take on the success principles discussed and watch your life and business transform and flourish.

Secrets of Building A Million Dollar Network Marketing Organization from A Guy Who's Been There, Done That And Shows You How to Do It Too.

With this book YOU will:
Get the six keys that unlock the door to success in Network Marketing.
Learn how to build your business free from doubt and fear.
Discover how the way you listen has limited your success.
Accomplish your goals in record time by shifting your listening.
Use the Zen of prospecting to draw people to you like a magnet.
Build rapport and find your prospect's hot buttons instantly.
Pick the perfect prospecting approach for you.
Turn any prospect's objection into the very reason they join.
Identify your most productive prospecting sources. And ...
Win the numbers game of network marketing.
Design a single daily action that increases your income 10 times.
Rate yourself as a top sponsor and business partner.
Create a passionate vision that guarantees your success.
And More!!!

"This is perhaps the best book available today on how to build a network marketing business."
— John Fogg, Founder *Upline*® Magazine

10 Weeks to Network Marketing Success: The Secrets to Launching Your Very Own Million-Dollar Organization in a 10-Week Business-Building and Personal-Development Self-Study Course

Learn the business-building and personal-development secrets that will put you squarely on the path to network marketing success. *10 Weeks to Network Marketing Success* is a powerful course that will grow your business with velocity and change your life!

With this course, YOU will:
Learn exactly how to set up a powerful 10-week action plan that will propel your business growth.
Learn how to prospect in your most productive niche markets.
Discover your most effective pathways to success.
Learn how to persuasively influence your prospects by listening to contribute value.
Build your business rapidly by making powerful requests.
Discover the secret to acting from your commitments.
Create a powerful life-changing structure for personal development.
See the growth that comes from evaluating your progress on a regular basis.
Learn how listening in a new and powerful way will skyrocket your business.
Uncover the secret to accepting complete responsibility for your business.

Learn how to transform problems into breakthroughs.
Develop the charisma that allows you to instantly connect with others on a heart-to-heart level.
Identify the secrets to stepping into leadership and being the source of your success.
And much more!

The *10 Weeks to Network Marketing Success* Program contains 10 weekly exercises on 4 CD's plus a 37-page workbook.

Restore Your Magnificence: A Life-Changing Guide to Reclaiming Your Self-Esteem

This book is *the* definitive guide to re-establishing your self-image. Dr. Rubino takes the reader step by step through the same exercises he has used to transform thousands of lives. The easy-to-understand exercises will become a roadmap to a life of happiness, fulfillment and self-esteem.

With this book YOU will:
Uncover the source of your lack of self-esteem.
Complete the past and stop the downward spiral of self-sabotage.
Replace negative messages with new core beliefs that support your happiness and excellence.
Realize the secret to reclaiming your personal power.
See how you can be strong and authentic. Use your vulnerability as a source of power.
Design a new self-image that supports your magnificence.

Realize the power of forgiveness.
Discover the secret to un upset-free life.
Re-establish your worth and reinvent yourself to be your best.
Create a vision of a life of no regrets.

"I have personally used this program's principles to support thousands of people to be self-confident, happy, and prosperous. You owe it to yourself to read this book."

— Dr. Tom Ventullo, President,
The Center for Personal Reinvention

Check your local bookstore or order directly from us.

ORDER COUPON

Yes, I want to invest in my future!
Please send me the following books or tapes by Dr. Joe Rubino.

Books	Price	Quantity	Subtotal
The Power to Succeed: 30 Principles for Maximizing Your Personal Effectiveness	$15.95	_____	_____
The Power to Succeed: More Principles for Powerful Living, Book II	$15.95	_____	_____
The Magic Lantern: A Fable about Leadership, Personal Excellence and Empowerment	$15.95	_____	_____
Secrets of Building A Million Dollar Network Marketing Organization from A Guy Who's Been There, Done That And Shows You How to Do It Too.	$17.95	_____	_____
Restore Your Magnificence: A Life-Changing Guide to Reclaiming Your Self-Esteem	$15.95	_____	_____
Secret #1: Self-Motivation (2 audio-tapes)	$39.95	_____	_____
10-Weeks to Network Marketing Success (4 CDs plus workbook)	$69.95	_____	_____
The Legend of the Light-Bearers: A Fable about Personal Reinvention and Global Transformation	$15.95	_____	_____
THE 7-Step Success System To Building a Million Dollar Network Marketing Dynasty	$18.95	_____	_____

MA residents add 5% sales tax
Shipping and Handling: ($3.95 U.S./Canadian orders; $9.95 non-U.S./Canadian orders)

Total _____

Name _____

Address _____

City State _____ Zip _____

Email _____

Telephone: _____

I'd like to pay by:
_____ Credit Card

Circle one:

      MasterCard   VISA   American Express

Credit Card Number _____

Expiration Date _____

Signature _____

_____ Check or Money Order Enclosed (US Funds Only)

_____ I am interested in learning more about The Center For Personal Reinvention's programs including coaching services.

Please place this order form with
payment into an envelope and mail to:
Vision Works Publishing,
PO Box 217
Boxford, MA 01921

www.ingramcontent.com/pod-product-compliance
Lightning Source LLC
LaVergne TN
LVHW091539060526
838200LV00036B/667